THE IMPOSTORS

Also by Timothy Balding

The Man Who Couldn't Stop Thinking: A Novel

THE
IMPOSTORS

TIMOTHY BALDING

A NOVEL

Upper West Side
Philosophers, Inc.

Upper West Side Philosophers, Inc. provides a publication venue for original philosophical thinking steeped in lived life, in line with our motto: philosophical living & lived philosophy.

Published by Upper West Side Philosophers, Inc. / P. O. Box 250645, New York, NY 10025, USA
www.westside-philosophers.com / www.yogaforthemind.us

Yoga for the Mind®

Library of Congress Cataloging-in-Publication Data

Names: Balding, Timothy, 1954- author.
Title: The Impostors : a novel / Timothy Balding.
Description: First edition. | New York : Upper West Side
Philosophers, Inc., [2019] |
Identifiers: LCCN 2018059602 (print) | LCCN 2019000605 (ebook) |
ISBN 9781935830634 (epub) | ISBN 9781935830627 (paperback :
alk. paper)
Classification: LCC PR9105.9.B35 (ebook) | LCC PR9105.9.B35 I47
2019 (print) | DDC 823/.92--dc23
LC record available at https://lccn.loc.gov/2018059602

A UWSP Original Softcover

When my love swears that she is made of truth,
I do believe her, though I know she lies ...

—William Shakespeare, *Sonnet 138*

CHAPTER ONE

Her husband had now been dead for a week. She still felt exhilarated.

Janet retreated deeper into the warmth of her bed and thought about Lady Macbeth. "*Come, you spirits that tend on mortal thoughts, unsex me here, and fill me from the crown to the toe top-full of direst cruelty!*" she exclaimed, rising slightly and thrusting out her arms dramatically.

She was boasting. She had not been able to be cruel to him, not much, anyhow, neither had she pushed him to murder, as far as she knew.

"Unsexed," on the other hand? Well, he had done a pretty good job for her there, she thought. Their physical life had petered out an age ago and she had never been able to cheat on him, even though he thoroughly deserved it, on the grounds of neglect, if nothing else. This could now be quickly fixed. She still felt attractive, really quite gorgeous sometimes.

Why was it, though, that Shakespeare's killers were exclusively men, she still wondered. She wished that she had stuck to her convictions and made the question the thesis of her literary degree. Her tutor had disapproved, saying it was dull and very 'passé'. She had thus gone on rather to perorate idly on post-traumatic stress disorder in Shakespeare's heroines. She had had a field day with Ophelia in this respect, it's true, but had been judged most unkind, totally lacking in sympathy for the spurned woman.

Yes, she still thought her subject highly interesting. The women had all either killed themselves—Cleopatra and her girl servant, Goneril, Juliet, Lady Macbeth herself, the pathetic Ophelia, Portia—or had been asphyxiated, stabbed, poisoned, or hung, like Desdemona, Lady Macduff, Cordelia, Emilia, Lavinia, Gertrude, Tamora, Regan … Not a good murderer of men among them.

Today, equality and women's rights would be demanded by the gatekeepers of literature and the theater directors, she thought. And quite rightly so! She had been thrilled to see a new production of Bizet in which Carmen had shot José. Good for her! She only faintly regretted making an idiot of herself by applauding. That was one of the few times in recent years that she had even managed to get him out of the house for the evening. He had not been impressed by the shooting and had hung his head in shame about her outburst, the fool.

She wondered whether she should go and take a last look at her José anyhow. (It was included in the funeral parlor's price, after all; three visits, no supplements). If he had been called José would it have changed anything? Or Manuel? Or even Jean-Pierre? Maybe not. In any case, he—indeed they—had been stuck with 'Ronald'. No wonder he had been unhappy.

It was wonderful to be alone in bed after all these years. To be able to splay out one's arms and legs at will without fear of colliding with a great hairy leg, fat belly or, God forbid, an invariably flabby penis and its attendant 'accoutrements', as she had liked to refer to them.

And above all not to have to pretend anything any longer. Yes, that was the essence of the freedom she now intended to enjoy to the hilt. For the others, of course, she would have to put on a show; that was obvious. Emotions were expected and had to be displayed appropriately. She had laughed at her own father's funeral and that had gone down very badly indeed, was still a talking point in the family. Even if it had been completely innocent: far too much brandy, a priest with a chronic stutter—"Our f-f-f-f-father, who art in h-h-h-h-heaven"—and genuine grief and confusion about losing her daddy.

Whether you loved or not the dear departed, their sudden absence was always at first a most mysterious existential shock. Like living in front of—well, what could she say? Windsor Castle?—and waking up one morning to find it was no longer there. No trace of it. Unlike other widows—God!, she detested that word and would not have it spoken in her presence—she had not had the experience of still expecting him, despite all reason and evidence, to suddenly walk in through the back door.

In any case, her first visit to the parlor, just the day after his body had been transferred there from the hospital, had temporarily shaken her. It was her first encounter with a corpse (she had not wished to see her father in this state) and it had been profoundly troubling. This wasn't José, or rather Ronald, at all. It was an unrecognizable slab of marble male, much like the effigies above the tombs of kings which had bored her so when she had been dragged around half the cathedrals of Europe as a child. If there was any connection between this thing and her late husband, she certainly couldn't see or feel it. A little to the surprise of the attendants, or whatever they were called, she had spent only a short moment with the body. It meant nothing to her. Even more a stranger dead than alive.

Turning over in bed and pressing her own, very much alive, body hotly against the mattress, she had a twinge, but no more than that, of guilt. She had at her disposal as many cheap sentiments as anyone else brought up in a reasonably civilized society, she thought, but felt strongly that, in the privacy of her own home, she had no obligation, for once, to make-believe. She had not loved him, not for several years at least—if ever—and was well shot of the whole farcical marriage game that they had been uselessly playing out into extra time and beyond.

Ronald had left no family that she knew of and his work colleagues had seemed to her very distant. So, in short, there was no one to mourn him and no one for whom she should feel sorry. Others would feel sorry for her, of course, but that was their business. She wished she could get past all that without an awful lot of fuss, but it seemed impossible. Well, that was the price she would have to pay for the charade she had organized about their relationship. And there was no use regretting that now.

I shall make it a good funeral, she thought; I'll send the old bugger out in style. That is what her own family—not to mention her friends—would expect, and she didn't want to let them down a second time. Her mother would most definitely scrutinize the coffin to see that she had not skimped on the price and would examine Janet's wreath, too, to make sure that it had come from only the best florist. Now she thought about it, her mother was probably the only person on earth who had loved Ronald. It's true that he was unfailingly kind and attentive to her, God knows why.

The buffet and the champagne (did one drink champagne at funerals?—she would have to check) must of course be first-class. Perhaps she could get drunk with her girlfriends after Ronald was soundly underground and her mother, brother, aunts and uncles had departed early to get back to their remote homes? Her friends wouldn't take it badly, most of them being excessive drinkers themselves. It might get maudlin, of course, but this most important act of the masquerade had to be played out well. She might even give them an apt burst of her Macbeth routine, which she often did at their weekly parties: "*After life's fitful fever, he sleeps well; treason has done his worst: nor steel, nor poison, malice domestic, foreign levy, nothing, can touch him further.*"

None of them had studied Shakespeare as she had and wouldn't know that these were words to attenuate and excuse a murder. They would only admire her for her oratorical skills and prodigious memory and for being such fun despite her sorrow. One of them might be tempted to make a joke about "malice domestic," but would probably hold her tongue. If there had been any "malice domestic" in her home, it had unquestionably come from him, in any case. Her friends would nevertheless certainly approve the escape from foreign levy, since most of them, like her, loathed those gangsters in Brussels. Only Ronald had been an ardent Europeanist.

In the early days of their marriage they had actually talked to each other about such issues. Europe, nuclear energy, globalization, the health services, climate change, the rise of populist movements, human rights in China; the kind of questions that all grown-up people should be concerned about. But they had agreed on practically nothing and these discussions had ceased very quickly to be enjoyable. It's only really fun talking to someone who has the same opinion as you, thought Janet. Otherwise life turns into a perpetual argument.

She was really looking forward to seeing her friends again, even though it had to be at a funeral. They had largely avoided her since Ronald's death, presumably thinking she needed to mourn alone. People invariably make the wrong choices in such circumstances, she philosophized. They either do too much or too little and really don't know which way to turn. If Sheila's husband had died, or Sally's or Veronica's, she'd have been right over to their places with a bottle of martini, a box of chocolates and a sackful of sympathy, she thought.

The sunlight through the bedroom window fell warmly on her breasts now and she quivered with pleasure. Ronald had banned her from taking off her bikini top when they sunned themselves on foreign beaches. "If you think I'm going to sit here calmly while all these bloody Frogs goggle at your tits you are gravely mistaken," he had raged on the very first day of their first holiday together when she undid her costume. She had been stunned. All around them, the French women were unthinkingly offering their breasts to the wind and she, the English woman, was forced by her husband to stay fully clad. "Bloody Taliban," she had protested, while covering herself again. Now, though, she was free to show her breasts to the whole world! "The beaches of Europe and beyond are waiting for my tits!" she exulted.

Yes, she must go and see him, or at least his body, once more. He had been naked the first time, though she had refused an offer from the funeral parlor to pull down the sheet (or was it a shroud? she wondered) and show the whole corpse to her. She had seen quite enough of that while he was alive. In the meantime, she had provided them with some of his clothes, which she hoped might give more meaning to him, might restitute a little of the man he had been, despite everything.

She found herself strangely at the crossroads of flippancy and gravity. Their marriage had failed dismally, that was certain. She had blamed *him*, made *him* responsible for their defeat, but at the end that no longer mattered, really. He had also been a human being floundering hopelessly on the shores of life. "Floundering hopelessly on the shores of life," she repeated her thought out loud. That was a pretty way to say it; perhaps reading so much Shakespeare had finally rubbed off on *her*. Maybe while showing her tits to the world she might also find time to write? She was sure that there was a novel in her, as there was in everyone, so it was said. Ronald had scoffed at the idea: "A novel in everyone? They should keep it there," he had retorted. It wasn't even original as a joke, she thought. He had certainly stolen it from one of the miserable, cynical writers he read while holed up in his study. Probably that Romanian he was always citing. What was his name? Cioran, yes, that was him. She had never read a word of the man and certainly never would.

But Macbeth, Macbeth ... It was her favorite of the Bard's plays, though she had never before asked herself why, as she did now. Perhaps because a woman gets men to do whatever she bids, even murder? She had never been in that happy position, had failed totally to budge Ronald from his catatonic state. She was proud, however, that she had finally given up trying to change him. Some women never did renounce. She wondered where they found their stamina and their undying expectation of eventual success.

"*Each new morn, new widows howl, new orphans cry, new sorrows strike heaven in the face*," she cried. It was surely so. But she would not howl (except perhaps at the funeral) and there was no sorrow in her. Quite the contrary.

CHAPTER TWO

Will was also in his bed, thinking about the day ahead.

He wondered what job the agency had in store for him. They had been rather cagey on the telephone and had merely said that they were diversifying their services and thought he might be the ideal man to launch their new 'product', as they put it.

Mike and his team were good people. He liked them a lot. They were ambitious, efficient, serious and caring and they paid promptly. They made sure their 'operatives', as they rather bizarrely called them, did a creditable job and, as in every good business, ensured afterwards that their clients were fully satisfied.

Will had stumbled across the Extra! agency nine months earlier on an Internet employment site for actors and models. The company said it was looking for people who were good at "role playing" and "improvisation" and "had experience"; with what they didn't specify.

Their address was in Soho, in Dean Street. The whole affair sounded rather shady, even though the district was no longer the hotbed of debauchery and crime that it once had been. But they had been very professional and kind when he called to make an appointment, and he had not thought twice about it when the receptionist said her name was Blanche. (He had since

got to know her. The name was not the best to have
when people called an unknown model agency in
Soho, she said, but she was fond of it. Vivien Leigh had
been the inspiration, after her mother saw the actress
play Blanche DuBois with Brando. Blanche adored
how 'Marlon' said her name and would encourage
agency operatives to try and imitate him. Will had so
far proved unsatisfactory in this respect. He was not
good at voice impressions; perhaps it was this that had
held back his career, he often thought).

In place of the narrow, seedy walk-up he expected
to find (he had not been back to Dean Street since slipping into strip shows there as a teenager), the Extra!
agency occupied the second floor of a spanking new
glass office building shared, as he observed from the
panel in the entrance hall, with accountants, lawyers,
an advertising agency, and a book publisher. Nothing
louche here, he thought with a twinge of disappoint-
ment.

"Welcome to Extra!—with an exclamation mark—
I'm Blanche, without an exclamation mark," said the
dowdy, bespectacled woman behind the reception desk,
smiling kindly. "How can I help you?"

"I'm Will Power—with no punctuation. I called earlier and you said, well, just to come on over. So here I
am, ready for role-playing and improvisation."

"You're funny, I like you," said Blanche. "Go over
there and take a seat and I'll let Mike know you're here.
He's the boss, the genius behind our organization. Only
he gets to hire people; he trusts no one else to do it.

Though he does occasionally ask for my opinion," she added with a sly wink.

He had only been sitting in the reception for a few minutes when he heard a voice boom, "Will-Power! *Your* parents must have had a sense of humor. Hahaha."

Will looked up to see an outstretched arm march across the hall, leading a very handsome and joyful young man in a fine three-piece suit. He didn't even have time to get to his feet before he found a hand firmly gripping and shaking his own.

"Mike, Mike Crophone!" announced the man loudly.

"Really?" asked a bewildered Will.

"No, no, just a joke! Willpower & Microphone, we would make a great act … Hahaha! Fielding, actually, Mike Fielding. But I do like playing with words, don't you?"

And without waiting for an answer or letting Will get his breath, he rushed on:

"Did you hear about the toucan who went to the supermarket to buy some fruit? The girl at the checkout asked him, 'Cash? Credit card?' 'No thanks', said the toucan, 'just put it on my bill'." To ensure he had been understood, Mike pulled a huge imaginary beak from his nose with his spare hand as he yanked Will off his chair with the other.

"Nice offices you have here," said Will as Mike dragged him a dozen yards by the arm before releasing him in front of a small conference room and pushing him inside.

"Glad you like them. Take a seat. The area is still a

bit steamy, of 'ill-repute' as they used to say, but it does-
n't appear to affect business. Dodgy characters have always plied their trade here—gangsters, drug pushers,
bent cops, whores, even Marx."

"Karl?" enquired Will, having just walked past The
Groucho Club down the street.

"That's the one," said Mike. "Do you know his
biggest problem?"

"Engels?" said Will hopefully.

"Haha! That's a good one. No, his problem was
here," said Mike, drilling a finger into his forehead.

"How's that?"

"No grasp of psychology, that was his problem,
didn't understand how we tick. Economics, history,
capitalism, revolution, sociology, even philosophy, yes
indeed—but no clue how the mind of the average man
works. Don't you think that's the problem of practically
all philosophers? Marx really had his head up his Hegel,
as far as I'm concerned. 'From each according to his
ability, to each according to his need'. Any idiot could
have told him that it would never work, that nobody
can function like that. Except with a gun in their
nuque, of course—most people readily accept the argument when it's presented to them that way."

※

Yes, Will remembered very well that first visit. The last
thing he had expected was to be lectured on Karl Marx's
failings in psychology and the nefarious effect of Hegel

on his theories about labor, but he had enjoyed immensely his first meeting with the boss of Extra!

"Tell me about yourself," Mike had asked.

"I'm thirty-five, live—alone—in Finsbury Park, work as an actor when I can, and between roles do bartending and waiting in restaurants. Hardly anyone can make a full-time job of acting, alas, as you well know."

"What kind of things do you do?"

"Well, I'll try my hand at most anything. I've done bit parts in TV series and occasionally get a run at the theater—mostly involving spears, if you see what I mean."

"Anything at the moment?"

"No, I'm back in the bar for the time being. But I trawl through the ads every morning. A real mixed bunch at the moment."

"Was there anything else today other than my outfit?" asked Mike keenly.

"Only one. I have it here actually, if you'd like to see it. I printed it, just in case."

With that, Will pulled a piece of paper out of his jacket pocket.

"Read it to me."

"Right: 'The plot: A man leaves his wife and child to take care of an injured chicken'," he began.

"I know how he felt," laughed Mike.

" 'Looking for a male actor who is Scottish or can put on a convincing Scots accent. He must also be able to sing and play the guitar in this short musical'."

"Haha! Gets better and better!" Mike snorted.

"'Please note that there will be a chicken on the set some of the time, so please do not apply if you are allergic to farm animals and chickens in particular'."

"Stop, stop, you'll kill me!" cried Mike, who was now wiping tears of laughter away from his eyes. "So, you're allergic to chickens? Hahaha! Priceless."

"No, I was OK for the chicken. The singing and the guitar, as well. But I don't think I can do a convincing Scottish accent, unfortunately. There's always some drawback."

"Do you know anything about Extra!?" asked Mike, sobering up and looking suddenly professional. "What does the name conjure up in your mind?"

"Well, I suppose you recruit extras …?"

"Very perceptive, my boy," said Mike, who was in his mid-twenties and thus a good ten years younger than Will.

"You know what's odd? I wasn't thinking about that at all when I found the name. It comes from my love of old crime movies. The scenes in which those little boys appear on the streets shouting 'Extra! Extra! Read all about it! Extra!' At which point, of course, the murderer throws the boy a nickel, grabs a paper, immediately sees his mug shot on the front page as the Wanted Man and then chucks it into the nearest garbage can."

Will had no thought at all about how to go on and simply sat there smiling. It was impossible not to warm to this man Mike and his stories and his enthusiasm, and whether or not this all came to something or not, he was having a good time.

"You're not a union man, are you?" asked Mike.

"Well, yes actually," replied Will apologetically. "I'd prefer that than looking forward to dying as a bartender. Is that a problem?"

"No, no, just curious. I read that if an extra says thirteen or more words during a scene he has to be contracted and paid as an actor. We don't abide by such rules, I'm afraid. And in our business, it'd be impossible anyway."

"Could you tell me more about this business of yours? Surely you don't interview all your extras personally?"

"Not for crowds, of course. There, we just line them up against a wall, a dozen at a time, holding number cards, like in a police identity parade. One or other of my colleagues asks a few questions, takes notes on their physique and attitude, and Bob's your uncle—'Goodbye, we'll call'.

"But we also have a lot of individual work, and there I like to make the selection myself. Because when I like someone and have faith in them I'm likely to be able to put a lot of work their way, and I really need to trust them."

"Do you hire mainly for film or the stage?" asked Will to show some initiative and get back into the conversation.

Mike grinned broadly, sat back in his chair, and winked.

"Neither. We only work in real life," he said without

further explanation, waiting for the effect of his words to sink in.

"I'm sorry, I'm not really with you ...," tried Will a little hopelessly.

"Then let's take a practical example," continued Mike. "You are not Will Power." He again paused for a reaction.

"Well I am, actually," said Will.

"So you say; but I don't know you from Adam. You certainly do a good job of being Will Power; you have the look and feel of Will Power; but I have no proof at all that you're the man. I can hardly ask you for your identity card, can I? Imagine that the real Will Power is lousy at interviews, or has a giant spot in the middle of his nose, or was born a hunchback, or simply couldn't get out of bed this morning, and that you've come in his place. It would work, you know. Even here, once a man is on our books, he doesn't have to show up often or at all. We just send him off on jobs from home."

Mike leant forward and said in a confidential tone: "So you see, we might hire a man who says he's Will Power but isn't and in fact be giving employment to a fraud, a total stranger! And if none of our clients complain, we'll never be the wiser. *You* could do an interview in the place of another man, don't you think?"

Like everybody looking for employment, Will had certainly fiddled grossly with the facts and created imaginary stage and screen experiences for his CV. But to send an impostor to do an interview in your place

… well, that was practically unbelievable.

"Do you get many assignments like that here?" asked Will incredulously.

"It's not our main line of business, but now the word's got around, we're seeing more and more. No one's been caught out yet and we've even landed a handful of jobs for our clients. It's getting easier and easier, now so many people work online from home. Outside the interview, you never have to show your nose in the office, so no one's the wiser that they've hired the wrong man."

"What other 'lines' are you in?"

"At the moment, politics is coming on very strongly, with the local elections in May."

"Not fake candidates, surely?"

"I hadn't thought of that — pretty difficult one to crack, I reckon," said Mike with clear regret. "You're catching on, though. Good idea. But no, supporters and hecklers; rather the latter, actually."

"Hecklers?"

"Yeah. 'Rubbish!', 'Get off!', 'Turncoat!', 'Bandit!', 'Thief', 'You kill me!', whatever. It's a rare art form, though. All a question of timing. A good loud laugh at the right moment can be devastating. Or a bit of wit. It's not for nothing that we advertise for improvisation skills. But I don't think you're the man for heckling."

"No? Why not?"

"It's become a bit rough. Practically any politician has a few gorillas in the hall now to deal with protesters. So we prefer to send lads who are a little physically intimidating themselves, if you see what I mean. Make the security people think twice or take long enough to pull them down and muffle them that they get in all their wisecracks anyhow.

"Did you read the Iliod?" continued Mike.

"The Iliod?"

"You know, the Greek thing, Troy, the horse and all that."

"Ah, the Iliad. No, I'm afraid not."

"Me neither. But I do my research, in my field that is. It turns out that it has the first recorded example of heckling. A bloke called, what was it … Thersites, I think, interrupts a pep talk by *Aga … Aga … Aga … mem … non*—phew, got that mouthful right, didn't I? —shouting that the Trojan war is about plunder and not honor and that the aforesaid is greedy and a coward."

"What happened to him?"

"Got clubbed unconscious. So you can see the dangers."

"You don't find me physically threatening then?" asked Will wryly. He prided himself on his good shape, his decent muscles, even his height, just over six feet.

Mike simply smiled and added: "Perhaps heckling about obscene management bonuses at a shareholders meeting or two. They're rather more genteel. And they don't expect it either, never see it coming."

"What, if anything, do you think I'd be good for, then?" asked Will.

"Friends and relatives," said Mike. "I saw it straight

away. Psychology, you know," he boasted once more, with the obligatory finger pointed again at his head. "You're a man people will trust without hesitation. Even Blanche has already given you the nod."

As nods go, that was pretty subliminal, thought Will, who hadn't noticed a thing.

"Sorry, but I don't understand. You're not saying that people hire friends and relatives, surely?"

"That's exactly what I'm saying, my son," said Mike, once more being paternal with the older man.

"Got the idea from Japan. People said that I was off my rocker. That we weren't half as screwed up in the head as the Japanese; that there would be no demand. And look at the result!"

At that, Mike stood up from the conference table and swept his arm panoramically around his empire, an open-plan office beyond the glass walls where two dozen people were sitting at desks gabbling into telephones.

"Impressive," said Will.

"Yes, the market was much bigger even than my vision told me; can hardly keep up with demand."

"But what kind of people look for friends and relatives at an agency?"

"All sorts," said Mike. "Our biggest demand by far is for boyfriends. You really wouldn't credit the amount of business we get in that direction. The city seems to be full of lonely hearts. No wonder the government's appointed a Minister of Loneliness."

"You're not talking about escorts, I suppose?" enquired Will with a disapproving grimace, even as he admitted to himself that such an idea might be quite appealing.

"Haha! No, we are absolutely not into that racket at all," rushed Mike to reassure him. "Perhaps I put it badly. I meant fake boyfriends. Others have cornered the market for dates and gigolos, and I wouldn't touch those things with a bargepole anyhow. I'm not a pimp. No, I'm talking uniquely about pretense. Laying a finger on the client is absolutely out of the question; it's a condition for staying with us.

"As I said, I got the idea from Japan, but I've adapted it to meet local circumstances, our different culture. Over there, believe it or not, lonely people hire friends because they don't know anyone who will listen to them, don't meet anyone with whom they can have a real conversation, a heart-to-heart. Everything's so formal, so rigid you simply cannot spout off about your feelings and problems and deepest thoughts, it's in very bad taste; you have to act as though everything's fine, whatever misery or confusion you find yourself in. But all humans need a good spout from time to time, I'm sure you agree. So they rent an attentive pair of ears and a soft heart for a couple of hours. It's caught on like wildfire, spread from Tokyo across the whole country.

"Here it's different. We wouldn't dare rent some one for a good chat, to pour out our souls; humiliating; we'd be far too ashamed of ourselves, at least that's my assessment.

"With that said, though, I've been thinking about

niches, specialization, with an educational angle to re-lieve the client of guilt. A good chat over a Greek salad with an Oxford literary prof about the life of Aga-what's-his-name, who pretends at the same time to be your friend, for example. For the moment, I don't think that I can crack the price barrier, though. Those dons make a good living."

"So, what *are* your girls after if not to pour their hearts out?"

"Well, in most cases I guess you could call it social acceptance. Put yourself in their shoes: you're invited to a party, or a girlfriend's wedding, or a day out in the country, have recently been jilted, divorced, aban-doned, or are frankly too hideous to find a man, and you want to put on something of a show for once, or even have the more modest ambition of avoiding at-tention and scrutiny. Girls can be terrible about sniffing out and interrogating their mates when they're in trou-ble—like the bloody Gestapo. Anyhow, where was I? Yes, so what's better for these jilted women—turning up alone, to be grilled or mocked or pitied or left in a corner, or to walk boldly and proudly into an admiring room on the arm of the handsome, strapping young Will Power? I rest my case, your Worship."

Mike hadn't rested his case there at all. He had gone on quickly to describe a wide range of scenarios involv-ing not simply girlfriends, but colleagues and family too. He was practically unstoppable, particularly when it came to exploring the psychological dimensions of the question …

Mike's parting remark, after he had announced grandly, "Welcome to Extra! You're hired!," and handed him back to the exquisite Blanche, had also remained firmly in Will's mind: "We don't do alibis, by the way. If you get even a sniff of a set up, you call me straight away."

＊

What a scheme, thought Will, grabbing a cigarette from the packet he'd thrown negligently to the end of his bed before sleep the previous night. What a scheme.

He had now done a couple of job interviews in the place of other men and had been amazed how far bluff and a little bit of Mike's cherished psychology could get you. He hadn't succeeded with either job, but Extra! didn't hold that against him, since the employment market was so tough and the agency's contracts did not have any guarantees on outcomes. Payment was due anyhow.

Both interviews had been for marketing posts. No other profession on earth was as nebulous as marketing or required fewer qualifications, and to put on a good show it was sufficient to keep your wits about you and throw in a handful of trendy words and expressions from time to time. Mike had advised him to say, very frequently, 'paradigm shift', à propos of everything and nothing, as in "This challenge clearly requires a paradigm shift." 'KPIs' and 'metrics' were pretty good too and should be included in the spiel from time to time when you didn't understand the question.

Chapter Two

Mike had been right. Shifting paradigms had been a fantastic success, combined, of course, with slightly more esoteric jargon like 'search engine optimization', 'link building', 'clickbait', 'conversion rates', 'engagement', 'digital mashups', 'retargeting', 'newsjacking', all of which Will was geared up to provide and exploit in abundance if they would hire him (or rather the coward who had rented him in order to avoid the interview). "And bla-bla-dee-dah," said Will out loud to himself.

He had not known what he was talking about. But these terms had clearly mesmerized and impressed the recruiters and in both cases he had made the job short-lists and, as far as he knew, just narrowly failed to clinch the posts desired by Extra!'s clients. So the agency felt its operative had done a good job.

Will dropped his burning cigarette into the remains of last night's wine in the glass on his bedside table and forced himself to quit the bed. His appointment with Mike was at eleven. That evening, he had another agency dinner date, a large family gathering; he wondered what the woman would be like this time.

He did not know then that the day would also be enriched by a meeting with the merry widow.

CHAPTER THREE

Janet had chosen the funeral parlor because of its promotional slogan: "We care, so you don't have to."

How marvelously appropriate, she thought. Yes, she would let Plum & Son take care of everything.

Plum the Elder was the very picture of a perfect funeral director. In unctuousness, obsequiousness, and sanctimony, he had nothing to envy Uriah Heep.

Janet adored people who had let democracy and egalitarianism pass them by and considered it their professional duty to humble themselves before their clients. There was far too little of that about these days.

Her model was Sartre's waiter. He was, in fact, the only single idea that she thought she had really grasped while wading through the swamp of *Being and Nothingness* in the philosophy option she had chosen by curiosity during her literary studies. Like every French waiter, he certainly considered himself to be immensely superior to his clients. His solicitousness was most certainly feigned; but *it did not matter*; it was completely the right way to behave. In public places, only *acts* count, she thought, not intentions or sincerity.

No, Janet wasn't looking for *authenticity* in people, God forbid. She had endured quite enough of that at home. The more bad faith the better, as far as she was concerned. The world was a show; she was now determined to play her part in it and expected others to do so too.

After all, if Ronald had given bad faith a try, had played the assiduous husband, things might have had a remote chance.

Wherever one went in life, one found caricatures, thought Janet, as a slightly agitated Plum père bowed deeply to her at the parlor door. One simply couldn't avoid them, nor should. It was all very well saying that everyone had his or her individual personality and temperament, but this undertaker resembled nothing so much as an undertaker in his every word and move, and that was exactly as it should be. Her butcher looked like a butcher too, florid cheeks and the stature of an immense beef carcass; her very garrulous, droll, effeminate and charming hairdresser was as such men should be; she had never seen her garagist without his filthy oiled-covered overalls and a spanner in his hand, talking incomprehensibly about valves and filters. Perhaps, like Sartre's waiter, they were playing at being a butcher, a hairdresser or a garagist; she had no idea, but doubted it somehow and really didn't care. It was all as it should be and immensely reassuring.

"Good morning, Madam," said Plum, practically folded in two in his welcome. She briefly feared the old man might never be able to stand upright again, so fixed did he appear in this posture.

"You have come to see the deceased once more?" he mumbled tonelessly into his belly.

No, I want to have a martini and talk about summer dress fashions, she thought to herself.

"Yes, I did call, you know."

"Dear me, young Plum must have forgotten to tell me," said old Plum, remaining in his bent position and waving his arms and hands out behind him like a chicken readying to take flight. "Dear me," he repeated, flapping his wings again in a covert signal to the two assistants who were lurking in the background that they should turn their heels and retreat from the vestibule into the back of the establishment. They eventually did catch on and disappeared.

"Please do take a seat in the waiting room. We'll have the thing ready for you in a jiffy."

The 'thing'? How quickly he passes from 'the deceased' to 'the thing', thought Janet. Even though on the basis of her prior visit she could hardly disagree with Plum that this was now the most appropriate description for what was left of Ronald.

The waiting room had evidently remained unchanged since the original Plum had fallen into the undertaking business in the late 19th century. Heavy dark-red velvet drapes adorned the windows; low, depthless mauve armchairs, into which one sunk at one's peril, never to rise again, perhaps, arranged in a circle around a central mahogany table on which lay a small selection of miniature brass coffins (perhaps ashtrays? wondered Janet; she certainly felt like a good puff); golden tassels in bunches hanging from everything.

The only interesting object in the room was a tall glass case housing a collection of urns to which the owners had helpfully affixed a bronze plaque labeled 'Cremation Over the Ages'. There was a very beautiful Egyptian bronze jar with the head of an inscrutable cat; a large, colorful Greek vase painted with scenes of a battle or an orgy, she couldn't quite tell which; a rather dull, simple, alabaster Roman pot; and a handful of more recent porcelain British urns, bereft of orgies, as befitted the temperate nature of the land's people, but with very pretty flower patterns. At the bottom of the case, in tiny and elegant script, someone had added a small cardboard notice: 'Reproductions'.

There would be no cremation for Ronald, though, no urn to choose for him. He had not confided much if at all to her on the conduct of his life, but on the matter of his death he had told her in earlier, more romantic days, when they, like everyone, had discussed such things to dramatize their love: "If ever I go before you, please don't cremate me."

He had then, inevitably, destroyed the poetry and pathos of the moment by ceding to his compulsion to explain everything about his feelings, on death in this instance. No, he did not want his ashes scattered over the Cotswolds or to lie in a pot on her mantelpiece. His ambition after life was to be feasted on by worms and slugs (or perhaps, he had said, worms might suffice because they ate the slugs anyhow), then carried off to their underground cities by ants and termites, one day perhaps to emerge into the light and be gobbled up by a partridge or pheasant.

Her husband's whole disgusting story had concluded, as she remembered, by birds being blasted out of the sky by gunshot and ending up on someone's dinner table. In this way, little bits of Ronald would survive in the stomachs of some jolly farmers or perhaps City bankers fond of game. Of course, that night or the next morning, as nature took its course in farmers' and bankers' bathrooms, the cycle would recommence ... "Stop!" she had cried. "Enough!" Ronald had been disappointed, quite irritated that she would not stay and hear the rest of his story of the eternal life that lay ahead of him on the condition that he be buried whole in the ground.

Soon enough, Plum reappeared. She noticed that he had brushed himself up a bit, rearranging as best he could the remaining strands of his white hair across his bald skull, and clearing the shoulders, sleeves and back of his black jacket of their dandruff drifts. To her great amusement, he had even put on a little red lipstick and some mascara and had powdered his cheekbones. Vanity, vanity, she thought. Or maybe it had come from a lifetime of trying to improve the aesthetics of corpses. He had simply turned the skill upon himself, perhaps out of habit.

Plum led her to the visitation room, as they called it, and shut the door behind her. 'Visitation', what a stupid word, she thought. Did they expect ghosts and spirits? The language was going to pot. Why not just 'viewing', or 'visiting'? No, everything nowadays must sound a little more elaborate than it really is.

Janet felt a chill in the air. Ronald had clearly just been dragged out of the freezer again, she thought. That's why they needed time; it wasn't only Plum's beauty session.

In contrast to her first visit, she sat down on the chair placed next to the coffin. Ronald had a little more color than before. The parlor had also pumped him with a new dose of formaldehyde to inflate his features a little and prevent him from looking too drawn.

"Hello, old bugger," said Janet. She wondered what he would reply if he could. He had liked it when she called him an old bugger; it was the closest thing to a term of endearment to have survived their shipwreck of a marriage in the last few years. In the very rare moments when they felt any residual affection for each other, or at least less hostility than usual, he would in turn refer to her as 'My old witch'.

"*Fair is foul, and foul is fair, hover through the fog and filthy air,*" she muttered to herself in remembrance of better times.

Ronald had enjoyed very much her outbursts of Shakespeare. It had probably been her undoing, she thought later. Why else marry a woman with whom you had little, if anything, in common? She had swept him off his feet with soliloquies and sonnets on their first dates, and he had quickly succumbed, barely protesting and unable to resist her ambition to drag him into rapid wedlock on the wings of her eloquence.

The first weeks and months of their life together had been as gloriously rich in words as a season at The Globe Theater. The old bugger had obligingly learnt swathes of Shakespeare in order to liven their dinner dialogues. At first he had drawn from the comedies and romances, seeking out the tender and raunchy, but as time went on Janet noticed the emergence of a distinct shift to the tragedies.

Now she recalled: He had even held up Hamlet to justify his desire to be consumed by worms, slugs, ants, partridges and bankers. Over a very fine turbot 'beurre blanc' she had cooked up one evening, he had suddenly proclaimed: "*A man may fish with the worm that hath eat of a king, and eat of the fish that hath fed of that worm.*" "It's still a disgusting idea, even if Shakespeare wrote it," she had retorted.

The efficient Plums had dressed Ronald in the pink shirt, flowery yellow tie, green Donegal Tweed jacket and black-and-white striped trousers that she had sent over. She had bought all of these things for him, mainly to assuage her guilt during shopping expeditions for herself; he had never worn any of them. "They're bloody clown's clothes," he had said of the ensemble, refusing to even try them on. It's a pity, she thought, he *does* look very smart dressed like this; he was quite wrong. She was happy that all these things had not after all gone to waste and that they would indeed be his only clothes in the after-life.

On rare occasions, reality resists any thought at all, is completely impervious to words and ideas. Janet leant

over the coffin and stared again at Ronald's stone imitation. She hoped that something profound and poetic
about existence might cross her mind to celebrate the
moment, but not a clever word, no word at all in fact,
came to her. She felt and thought absolutely nothing.
She was only anxious to get back out into the sun and
clear her nostrils of the foul stenches of death. She
should not have come.

CHAPTER FOUR

"**D**o you weep easily?"

"I do, actually," replied Will.

"I could have sworn it," said Mike proudly. "Psychology," he added, pointing as usual to his head.

"I'd surely cry even at a complete stranger's funeral."

"Odd you should say that," said Mike. "I don't know how you do it, frankly. Personally, I never cry at all, and even less could I do it on demand."

"On demand?"

"I'll come back to that. But tell me how things are going, I haven't seen you for ages. Do you enjoy working with Extra!? We've had nothing but glowing reports about you, I must say. I think my judgement of your character and abilities was spot on. I like getting things right in that department, I admit."

Will smiled and in turn indicated his forehead.

Mike nodded. "Exactly."

"Well, I think I can say that the last nine months have been among the best of my life," Will said honestly and earnestly. "I've adored working for the agency."

"Perhaps you should be paying *me*," laughed Mike. "I'm delighted to hear it, though."

"At first, I felt a bit of a fraud, I have to confess. You know, ethical qualms and doubts about deceiving people. But soon something rather odd happened."

"Yes?" said Mike eagerly, leaning forward over the table.

"I'm not quite sure how to put it really. I soon began to feel more honest and truly myself while playing these rôles than in the moments when I was back in my 'real' life, such as it is."

"Fascinating," said Mike in expectation that his already very developed skills in psychological analysis were about to enter new, unexplored territory. "What do you mean?"

"It's pretty paradoxical, I know, but in real life I feel obliged, like everyone, I suppose, to don some mask or another, to promote an image, I guess ..." His thought trailed off into silence, but Mike urged him on by thrusting out his hands and revolving his fingers upon themselves.

"It's confession time, then, Father Fielding?" laughed Will.

"No, no, just professional interest, refining my perceptions and my knowledge of the human soul."

"All right. Is the Mike Fielding sitting here in front of me the same Mike Fielding I would see if I was a fly on the wall at his family dinners, for example?"

"Never thought about it, to tell the truth."

"Well, without offense, I would guess that you are playing a different persona in each environment. Mike the boss here. At home, Mike the husband, Mike the father."

"Mike the Holy Ghost," continued the Extra! boss. But he didn't much like his integrity being examined and questioned in this obscure manner and rapidly pushed Will to return to himself as the subject. Psychology was fine as long as it was exercised on the others, not oneself.

"Perhaps I am all such personas, as you put it," said Mike. "But as 'Mike the boss', I'd prefer that you told me more about your own experience, as you started to do."

Will acquiesced, having had a moment to recollect his thoughts about his brief life with Extra!

"Well, let me give you an illustration of what I'm getting at. Imagine standing alone in a bar and being accosted by a curious and impertinent, half-sloshed stranger, who asks aggressively 'What do *you* do, then?' It happens to me all the time. I apparently look like a man open to approach.

"I don't know what *you* do on these occasions, but I usually say that I'm a space ship test pilot, or an escaped convict, or, with my best Germanic accent—that one's easy—that I'm Herr Professor Doctor Doctor Fuckemall of the Viennese Institute of Quantum Psychology, or somesuch. This generally blocks their fudged minds for a few minutes; but they come back at you, of course, because there's no one on earth as relentlessly nosy as a drunk. They're all the same; they simply never give up, keep repeating themselves, the same questions. Broken records.

"The other night, I even had one of them ask me the inevitable question while I was at work, behind my *own* bar. 'What do *you* do, then?' I was saved from having to point out the absolutely bloody obvious when he conveniently fell off his barstool and out of sight. He was then dragged out and dumped on the pavement by my colleague Paul, who is a combination bouncer-waiter, a rare talent."

"Doctor doctor, you said?"

"Yes, the Austrians really do say that when a man has two PhDs. I even know an academically brilliant shrink with four doctorates who insists on being called Doctor Doctor Doctor Doctor Strumpf, at least when he's in Vienna. He told me — he's an habitué of my bar —that he regularly gets five 'Doctors' from people who can't speak and count at the same time. Once, even six! Unbelievable. My suspicion, though, to be honest with you, is that Herr Strumpf is not a Doctor at all, not even once, but an impostor—like me. I think perhaps he's on the run from an asylum. But I can never be sure, you know how it is.

"Anyhow," continued Will, "I find the moment after the first sally with the drunks to be really interesting. I could make up any number of extravagant stories to keep the poor devils amused, but why should I? I don't owe them anything. Why should I pay for the entertainment of the inebriated?"

"So, what *do* you say then?"

"I tell them the truth. The pure, undiluted truth about my existence in all its excruciating banality and poverty. And do you know what? This has two bene-fits: Firstly, it gives me a wonderful occasion to catch up on my life and my articulation of its complete emptiness in front of an imbecile who can barely grasp my words through his soggy mind and will forget everything well before the end of the evening; and secondly, that the drunken gentleman in question will find me so incredibly tedious that he will eventually turn away, crushed with boredom even in his alcoholic stupor, and pick on some other poor bastard to berate and interrogate."

"Fascinating," repeated Mike.

"And so it has been with my Extra! jobs. Exactly like the bars. A little pretense and a lie or two at the outset —'Yes, Shirley and I have known each other for several weeks now'—and then just the truth, my whole life honestly set out in front of them all in the certain knowledge that I shall see none of them ever again. No effort, no subterfuge of the kind we are obliged to employ at every turn in our day-to-day existences. It's a piece of pie, Mike. And I'm really getting to know myself better in the process, because a man advances in life by forever refining his own narrative, don't you think?"

"Fascinating," said Mike for the third time in the discussion, all the while ignoring the question, which he found incomprehensible.

"I do enjoy these chats, Will, we should do this more often. But now I think we have to get down to the business in hand, your latest job. Let me cut to the chase: You are going to be our very first mourner, a line in which, if you do a good job, I see a very great future for both of us."

In a conspiratorial tone and with much extraneous and invented color, Mike explained that he had been visited at the agency the previous day by a beautiful, classy, enigmatic lady, who needed an Extra! extra for a funeral.

"I finally got to play Philip Marlowe. My dream!" said Mike with joy, recounting the encounter.

"This mysterious dame walks unannounced into my office, a spectacular yellow cartwheel hat tilted on her head—Jesus, I wish I had been wearing my Fedora—sits down without invitation on the edge of my desk, pulls up—just slightly—her skirt above her knees, draws deeply on a cigarette and asks huskily through a cloud of smoke: 'Do you do funerals?' I thought at first she wanted us to plug some one! I replied — and here I was *really* cool Will: 'Well, we don't make 'em *happen*, if that's what you mean'.

"She was 'a really gorgeous broad, a redhead'," added Mike, trying and spectacularly failing in his imitation of Bogart, despite drawing his upper lip up over his teeth in a scowl.

"But she wasn't asking us for a hit job, after all. She needs someone to play her late husband's greatest pal at his funeral."

"Why can't *he* do it?"

"He doesn't exist, apparently. But I really don't know much more. She was rather tight-lipped about the whole question and I don't press our clients when it's not necessary. It's *your* job to explore all that. And because of this, the assignment will be longer than usual. She said money wasn't a problem. So give it three or four days at least, but come back to me if you need more than that. OK?"

As Will got up to leave, Mike asked him: "Did you know the Chinese have strippers at their funerals?"

Will laughed in anticipation of another one of Mike's good jokes, but he was apparently serious.

"Really. Strippers drive up attendance, as one can well imagine, and large crowds are considered a mark of honor for the defunct and evidence of affluence. Rich families also hire pole dancers and comedians, even singers, to show off their wealth. Incredible, no? I was wondering how all this could be brought to London, but somehow I don't think it would fly. Sure to be arrests. 'Come, come, young ladies, please put your clothes back on and accompany us down to the station'. No, for the moment Extra! will have to stick to fake mourners. That's a pretty good start."

In front of the reception on his way out, Will lowered his eyelids, raised his head, thrust out his lower jaw and mumbled "Show long Blaensshh" through his teeth.

"No, you idiot, that's Don Corleone, not Stanley Kowalski. You're mixing your Marlons. Go away and practice a bit more. Bloody hopeless," said Blanche, raising her eyes to the ceiling.

CHAPTER FIVE

"**A**fternoon, I'm from the Extra! agency."

"Ah, so you're Fred."

"The name's Will, actually."

"No, you're Fred. I'll explain later. Please come on in."

Janet Chapman's house, now really *her* house, as she had begun to tell herself, lay in a terraced Regency cul-de-sac just off Kensington High Street. It was not an area that Will frequented very much.

Painfully polite as always, he felt compelled to say "Nice house!," a remark Janet ignored as she led him in to the ground floor salon and indicated an armchair.

"Would you like a drink?"

Will looked stupidly at his watch as if it was the arbiter of whether he might feel like a drink or not and said: "Great, yes please, I'd love a scotch. If you have one." Three-thirty or not, it's true that he needed a slight lift.

Janet soon brought his glass and the bottle too. She had made a giant gin and tonic for herself in a kind of bulbous vase.

"I understand that you're an actor." And before he could protest: "Have you ever done any Shakespeare?"

"I once played Birnam Wood."

"How wonderful! You were a tree?"

"I played the whole forest, actually. Low-budget

47

production. Dragging branches back and forth across the stage for three weeks. Couldn't get the smell of pine out of my nose for months afterwards. Not to mention all the pine needles stuck in my clothes."

"Pine? They should have been oak!"

"Small budget, as I said. Someone had the bright idea of recycling used Christmas trees. It was a New Year production."

"How marvelous that you appeared in *Macbeth* at all, even as a wood! *Who can impress the forest, bid the tree unfix his earthbound root* ... I so envy you. *Sweet bodements!* I'm so jealous."

And in a moment of arch silliness, she thrust out her bent and twisted arms and imitated a disgruntled tree, not from *Macbeth*, but from ... *The Wizard of Oz*, perhaps?

Am I being a little too coquettish? wondered Janet. Christ, I have such a desire to flirt now, even with total strangers. I must restrain myself. There will be time. A whole new life. Don't rush it, even though this Will does look like a very nice boy and not at all the kind who might take advantage of a wantonly forward woman.

"Ice?"

"No thanks, it's just great as it is."

"Let's get down to business then," said Janet.

"Indeed."

"Well, it's like this. My husband Ronald knocked himself off a week ago. A heart attack provoked by an overdose. Sleeping pills, apparently. He'd been taking them for a couple of years. I found an empty box."

"I'm so sorry."

"No, we can skip the sympathy and condolences, don't worry. As a hired hand, you don't have to pretend anything at all. Not to me at least. Your acting talents will only be required at a later moment. You are not yet Sartre's waiter."

A hired hand? Not the nicest thing I've ever been called, but she's right. Sartre's waiter? What on earth did that mean? He kept his silence.

"So what did your boss tell you?"

"He reckoned that you were 'a very mysterious dame'," said Will, imitating well Mike's poor imitation of Humphrey Bogart.

Janet threw back her head and its shock of red hair in pleasure and laughter and lit a cigarette.

"He was a private detective for a couple of years," Will explained. "A frustrated Sam Spade who didn't find the glamour he was looking for. Just sordid divorce work, following wayward husbands and freezing on street corners. So he ended up in an office. But at least it's his own office, he says. And it seems you made him feel like Spade or Philip Marlowe for ten minutes and brought back his early fantasies."

"How lovely! I do quite see myself as a femme fatale, it's true," said Janet as sultrily as she could, regretting her confession instantly. "Hold yourself, girl, hold yourself," she muttered into her gin vase.

"So, yes. Ronald shuffled off his mortal coil a week ago. They're taking good care of his corpse at Plum &

Son, an old-fashioned and distinguished house of death in Belgravia. Unfortunately, the police or the coroner —I'm frankly not sure which—won't release the body yet so Ronald can start his death properly and we can all get on with our lives. I've left all this nonsense to Plum junior, who will tell me when we can fix the funeral date. He has some legal training, apparently."

"And where do I come in? Mike was very short on detail. It seems you want someone to play your husband's best friend. Is that it?"

"Yes." And without asking, she rose, took the bottle of scotch from the salon table, and gave Will another good shot. "It's a long story which I shall endeavour to make short."

Janet said that she and Ronald had been married for ten years—"though the last two or three seemed like a hundred."

She would not dwell on their early years together. That had nothing to do with the task at hand, and she guessed that Will wouldn't find it particularly interesting either.

He shrugged his shoulders politely and smiled.

"But at one stage, a year or so ago, Ronald became a little sullen, often abandoning our dinner discussions in mid-course and shutting himself in his office, where he would remain long after I had gone to bed. He was scribbling, apparently.

"I tried to talk to him about it, ask whether things were going badly at work, or if he was suffering a bit of depression, or whatever, but he had nothing helpful to say at all. He just kept on withdrawing further into himself and further away from me. When we quarreled about it, all he could say was, 'You don't understand!' — as if I could when he wouldn't tell me anything, give me any clues.

"Until he started cracking, Ronald and I had enjoyed a very active social life. I just *adore* parties and dinners and dancing, and at first he seemed to love these things too. He was one of the very few English men who can dance without looking like a complete idiot; real rhythm, a good mover. He was also knowledgeable and very witty and would shine at dinner discussions. Everybody liked him, particularly my close girlfriends, all of them great flirts; I even suspect they preferred him to their own husbands, but I felt proud about that and forgave them easily. For he was mine.

"Got to get another drink, please excuse me," said Janet suddenly, rising and disappearing.

Will took the opportunity to examine the room. It was very elegantly furnished, in Regency style to match the house. What struck him, though, were the large number of frameless photographs in all shapes and sizes sitting on various tables, shelves, chests of drawers and the marble mantelpiece; a few were also pinned crudely to the walls.

Janet took time to return, so Will got up and wandered around the salon to peer at the pictures. Practically without exception, they featured a fine-looking, sturdy man, arm in arm and hand in hand with Janet, as well as alone on a horse, walking through woods with a rifle, or hanging on to large fish with his rod on a boat. Quite a sportsman, thought Will; how *do* the other half live.

"Quite a gallery, hey?" said Janet as she re-entered the salon clutching at her refilled vase. "I've spent the last couple of days sorting them out. They're for the wake — though I'm not sure that's the right term, since the party will be after the funeral. The only problem is that you are not in any of them; but we're going to fix that."

"What do you mean?"

"We'll talk about that later; but to go back to my story. One day, for no good reason, Ronald told me at the last moment that he couldn't join me at a birthday party for one of my closest friends—Sheila, you'll see her at the funeral. He obstinately refused to say why and just insisted I should tell the gathering that he was sick. And so I did. I went on my own and came back bearing sympathy and get-well messages for the *malade imaginaire*.

"He accompanied me to various occasions after that, but then one day he announced that he would go out no longer for 'these stupid, futile evenings of mental depravity', as he called them. I tried to reason with him; asked him to do it for *me*, if nothing else; said we must put on a show from time to time for the sake of decency; even tried to make him jealous by telling him I was a great flirt when he wasn't around; nothing would budge him. Our shared social life was over, like several other things in our marriage by that time. And that's when Fred appeared."

Janet sighed deeply and delicately swept a tear away from under one eye with a brightly painted fingernail. She felt a little Shakespeare coming on, but valiantly resisted it.

"Excuse me. It's the gin. Nothing else at all. I always get emotional with gin. It doesn't happen at all with other drinks, not with wine for instance; quite odd that. Where was I?"

"The appearance of Fred."

"Ah yes, indeed. I have my pride you know. Quite a lot, actually. The first few times that Ronald refused to come with me, I continued to invent illnesses, work obligations, the odd trip to Frankfurt. But I really could not bring myself to say that Ronald didn't want to be with me and wanted even less to spend his time with them, the 'mentally depraved'.

"There were no doubts or suspicions that I could see, just regrets all round. But I increasingly felt that we must find a more durable solution. So I sat down with Ronald one evening and asked him to help me. He came up with the idea. He put it like this:

"'Tell them that my best, closest friend—let's call him Fred — is going through a very painful divorce, that he's suicidal, in fact, and that I must spend practically all of my spare time with him, to save his life perhaps.

"I thought that was a bit summary as a story; Ronald told me to use my 'considerable imagination', as he put it, to embellish it. And that's what I did. I not only invented Fred-the-dear-old-friend and Fred-the-rejected-husband and Fred-who-wants-to-kill-himself, I began to give him other attributes and indeed a whole life. He's an alpine climber, you know."

"Really?" said Will. "And the story of his divorce?"

"He's been married for ten years, happily at the beginning, like most of us; but gradually his wife withdrew into herself, shut herself away in her study, began to write novels, neglected even to be polite to him, more often than not slept in a separate bedroom and one day announced she had a lover.

"As you see, I don't have as much imagination as Ronald claimed; I just told my story in reverse—except for the lover, of course. There was no other woman in Ronald's life.

"And finally, the poor man did try to kill himself, despite Ronald's care and attention," said Janet guiltily.

"I guess I should know how?"

"I was a bit lacking in inspiration there. I should have said that he threw himself down a crevice on the Matterhorn, but landed safely, cushioned by a ridge of deep soft snow. But I just said that he slit his wrists, I'm afraid. So make sure that you wear long sleeves at all times on this job. Because I know my inquisitive friends ..."

Will wondered whether he should start taking notes. He'd certainly have to look up the names of a few mountain peaks.

"Don't worry, I'll tell you more about Fred in a day or two, when I've had a chance to collect my thoughts and remember all my lies. In the meantime, it's even more important that you, as his closest friend, should get to know Ronald. But there, I think I have a solution. Hold on a moment."

With that, she walked out of the room and he heard her climbing up the wooden stairs to the next floor of the house.

"Well here's another fine mess you've gotten me into," said Will out loud to himself, trying on Oliver Hardy's voice and failing to quite get it.

This job might even live up to Mike's excitement about the dame, he thought. He had squirmed a little when she had said that Ronald had "knocked himself off," thinking it unnecessarily crude and gratuitous; but it was not in his nature to judge people. Not when they're hiring me, he thought, quickly correcting this cynical slur on his own character—he judged nobody, in fact.

Janet was bearing a yard-high stack of notebooks in front of her when she reappeared.

"Voilà. His diaries. At least he did something while shut away all those evenings in his study."

She flung them down unceremoniously on the floor in front of Will and exclaimed: "*Make me a willow cabin at your gate, and call upon my soul within the house. Write loyal cantons of contemned love, and sing them loud even in the dead of night.*"

"Twelfth Night, as you, the actor, must know," said Janet, drunk with poetry, a sense of the loss of something—perhaps an ambition of love—and, above all, two immense glasses of gin.

"Have you read them?" enquired Will.

"No!" said Janet with great conviction. "Nor shall I ever!"

She only added, with not a little passion:

"Understand this, Fred. I want to be, I *must* be, the woman who had a gloriously happy marriage, the sublimest marriage you could possibly even dream of. I will not be the victim, I will not be condemned for ever to sly whispers in room corners and pitying, or perhaps even malicious, words and looks. I can put on a bloody good show, don't doubt it. And you must put on a bloody good show to help me. I'm just trying to figure out a way to keep his death an accident; I guess no one will broadcast that he did himself in. We'll see. In fact, I've only told my mother that it was suicide. She deserved to know and will keep it to herself. But anyhow, these diaries, whatever they say, do not exist, if you catch my drift. They are now your secret alone."

He wondered if he should discuss this last point with Mike. He supposed it wasn't necessary; no crime was suspected, after all.

❋

Will found himself back in Kensington High Street carrying a small brown suitcase laden with a suicide's diaries. For the moment, his greatest problem was to decide what to do with this load. He was due to meet his new Dulcinea in two hours and calculated that he couldn't possibly get back to Finsbury Park and then return to Battersea in that time. Could he show up with a suitcase? No, that really wouldn't do.

CHAPTER SIX

In plain English, she was fat. He wondered how one expressed this correctly in our days. 'Weight handicapped'? No, that sounded like a steeplechaser. 'Weight challenged' perhaps?

An immense grinning blonde waddled menacingly across the pub towards him. Since they were the only people in the establishment, they knew that they were destined for each other.

He rose to his feet, smiled, offered his hand and said: "Hi. I'm Fred … Sorry, I mean Will."

"You're Charles, in fact."

They both laughed.

"I'm Mary. Get me a drink, would you. A Bloody Mary, of course. And whatever you want. Here."

Delving into her purse, she handed him a bank note. Having women buy drinks and cover other expenses was something he had been obliged to get used to working for Extra!, even though it was completely against his nature and pained him. He would otherwise be quite out of pocket on these jobs and he did have his rent to pay.

"Is this *your* suitcase?" Mary asked with a grimace of distaste as he returned with their glasses.

"Yes, I'm afraid so," said Will, shoving the valise further under the table with his foot to show her that he disapproved of it at least as much as she.

"Fancy bringing a suitcase with you on a date! You're a weird one."

"I'm sorry, really. But I got stuck with it on another job which ended late and couldn't figure out what to do with it. You can't leave these things in stations any longer, you know; could be a bomb."

"But what *is* inside?"

"A dead man's diaries."

"You *are* weird, definitely," said Mary.

They had arranged to meet for an hour, to get their stories accorded, before going on to the party.

"So, what *is* our story?" asked Will.

Mary sniggered. "You bumped into me in a street in the West End …"

How could I miss, thought Will, immediately castigating himself for his facile cruelty.

"… throwing me towards the ground, all the while grabbing my knockers in a vain attempt to keep me upright. You apologized profusely while running your hands up and down my body to brush off the dirt from the pavement. I protested weakly at all this fondling as I sank into your arms. We've never looked back."

"So, love at first grope? That's it? A fine, moving story indeed.

"Who'll be there tonight to hear this edifying tale?" asked Will.

"It'll be half family and half friends. Our host will be my evil sister—we loathe each other. They'll be her husband, a couple of their friends, my two brothers and their spouses and a few of their friends too. About twenty in all, I'd say. I hope they'll be a free bloke or two."

Absurdly, Will felt a twinge of hurt at her ambitions about available men. I'm a human being too, he laughed privately.

"Could I ask why you rented a man for the evening?"

"My sister has mocked me about guys since we were teenagers; she always got the pretty boys, and I was always left with the gormless nerds. I wasn't always fat, you know, but even at that time she had an edge on me."

"You're not fat." Will wondered how the words had found their way out of his throat.

"Lying sod!" laughed Mary. "But keep it up; that's what I'm paying you for."

"You said your sister always had an edge on you anyhow?"

"Yes, I don't know why. Well, I do actually. She's prettier, wittier and quite shameless."

"Shameless?"

"No hesitation about going for it. Despite what you might think, the women with most success in our days are not those who insist that men perform some kind of peacock fan dance for them. It's those who see what they want and grab it by the balls—literally or otherwise—who get the goods.

"We can still con practically any man into marriage," she went on. "We have the upper hand psychologically, as was always the case, probably because we understand life so much earlier than you do. We throw our nets over you before you even know what's happening. Men are still trying to figure out what's going on, using what passes for their reason, while we're laughing ourselves down the aisle. If you ask me, that's why marriages on the whole don't last very long these days. Most of the conned do eventually wake up to the fact that they've married the wrong women, and vice versa of course. But God how slow you guys are."

Well, that was quite an indictment of the male, thought Will. Never happened to me, though. Here I am at thirty-five and no woman has ever tried to cast her net in my direction, not that I have observed, in any case. Perhaps indeed I just haven't noticed? It's true, now he thought about it, that one girl had accused him of being 'totally blind' about women, her in particular. He hadn't understood what she was talking about, but perhaps Mary had given a clue. He really couldn't figure out the whole business.

"Perhaps we should know a few things about each other, true or otherwise," Will suggested.

"You first."

"Right. I'm single, obviously; I was born in Crouch End, and now live in Finsbury Park. To those who might say I haven't gone very far, I must boast that I did once have a room in East Finchley. I went to a local school until eighteen but didn't do university and instead took a job in a bar in Chelsea. My ambition was to become an actor. I am one, actually, though work is difficult to get, and I still have to play the bartender more often than not, currently in Islington. So, there isn't an awful lot to remember, frankly. And beyond that, I guess that no one there tonight will have the slightest interest. And you?"

"What kind of acting jobs? What films or plays have you been in?"

He explained, as he had now done with a dozen other clients, all of whom imagined indescribable glamour and glitz in this stage and cinema life, that he was a bit-part man who hadn't even ever made the credits, though he still lived in hope. She wouldn't have heard of any of the titles he was in.

"We're going to have to invent something, Will my boy, make it look better than that. I did tell Sonya—my sister—that you were an actor, and she was practically speechless, which is a rare thing for her. Like everybody else, she's obsessed with the lives of movie stars and will certainly grill you about these things. I can't be going out with a loser."

They sat in silence for a minute or two.

"Do you speak French?" asked Mary suddenly.

"Mais oui, Madame, bien sûr. I can get by, at least."

"Fantastic. We'll say that you specialize in playing Englishmen in Frog cinema. Nobody ever watches French films, so you can concoct whatever you like without fear of recognition or contradiction. You go to Paris to make them, by the way. Go easy on East Finchley and Finsbury Park. They really don't fit the bill, you know."

Mary in turn sketched out a life. Just enough to cover what a man might reasonably expect to know about his girlfriend after a few weeks together. She had been married once to a man everyone had disliked from the start; with reason, she had come to see.

"It's amazing how we can make mistakes about people," she told Will. "It's not so much that we are 'blinded with love', or crap like that, but rather that we accept the image that a person projects about himself —or herself, I suppose. Everyone else thought that he was a goofy creep; they all warned me against him. And they were right—he was a complete toad. I simply can't understand how Sonya or anyone else saw through him while I didn't. I can only suppose that I saw what I wanted to see whereas the others had no interest at all in seeing anything else than the reality. And they were right, the bastards. The fawning toad turned out to be a complete phoney. All the interest he showed in me and my life and my thoughts turned out to be completely bogus. The only thing that I haven't grasped even to this day is *why*. Why did he pretend all that? With what objective? Marriage is insane, don't you think?"

Will had no view at all on marriage, though his most recent Extra! encounters were certainly confirming that it was not a straightforward matter.

In genuine sympathy for this nice, troubled woman, he laid a hand on her arm and smiled compassionately.

"Hands off, Will!" she exclaimed, laughing. "I could have you fired! Hahaha! I've read my Extra! contract, you know. It says that if any 'operative' — that's a weird expression, isn't it?—lays a finger on me, I am invited to immediately inform the agency, for full reimbursement of my advance and disciplinary action against you."

Will laughed.

"Anyhow, I don't suppose that any of your family would have the bad taste to talk about your former husband in the presence of your new boyfriend, though," he said confidently.

Mary laughed in a disabused kind of way. "You don't know my family. You have no idea, simply no idea."

It sounds though it might be an interesting evening, thought Will.

❋

Sonya made her way slowly and circuitously through the room towards Will with all the subtlety and guile of a carnivorous flower closing on its victim. He knew perfectly well that he was the creature destined to be devoured and took a large gulp of whisky to embolden himself for the confrontation ahead.

Mary had not entirely forgotten Will, either; she had already trapped a male guest in a corner, blocking any possible escape route for the poor man, while simultaneously throwing wicked smirks to Will over her shoulder and jerking her head in the direction of her sister as she snaked her way towards him.

Will smiled to himself and enjoyed for a moment an overwhelming sense of well-being. What a life! he thought. So much more rewarding than the scripted stories of the stage or the television. *This* is for real, even though it is fake. How could that be the case? he wondered.

Will's nascent philosophical musings were happily brought to an abrupt halt by a short skirt and shapely pair of legs which had stopped in front of the canapé on which he was sitting and were clearly demanding his attention.

He looked up at Sonya as she looked down upon him. "May I join you?" she asked.

"By all means! Have a seat. Nice party."

"So, it's Charles, isn't it?"

He nodded and smiled.

"Charles what, may I ask?"

He and Mary had neglected to decide on this detail.

"Charles Acton."

"I thought you said Charles 'Actor' for a moment. That would have been very droll, wouldn't it?" she giggled.

"Indeed, indeed. It's Acton, though."

"Mary tells me you're in movies," said Sonya, patting his thigh and snuggling up just a little closer in evident wonder at this opportunity to touch a real, live screen star in the flesh.

"Indeed." I'll have to do better than that, he thought, and volunteered: "Yes, you wouldn't have seen any of them, unfortunately. All French. None of them have been distributed over here."

"What was the last one called?"

"'L'Escargot Qui M'aimait'," said Will without missing a beat. Where the devil did you find that idiocy? he challenged the malicious scriptwriter of his thoughts.

"And what does that mean?"

"The Snail Who Loved Me," regretted Will.

"What on earth is that about?"

"It's a psychological drama about an Englishman who moves to Burgundy to breed snails for the British market."

"I didn't know that there *was* a market for snails here," Sonya interjected. "We hate the slimy things, don't we?"

Good at improvisation, that's what Mike had hired him for …

"Quite so! That's precisely the drama. Here he finds himself, overrun with snails that no one wants to buy. The French won't touch them—perhaps because they were brought up speaking English—and the British send him packing."

"Snails who speak English?"

"That was a joke. Not a very good one, I admit. But anyhow, left with hundreds of snails that no one wants, and which he cannot personally eat for sentimental reasons, he gets to know and befriend them. One in particular. A kind of queen snail, as it were; a real leader. Every one lives happily ever after. Or should have, because his restless imagination soon dreams up a scheme to breed frogs for Britain; we don't eat those either, of course, which emphasizes the tragic dimension of the tale."

"That's all very weird," said Sonya, as Mary had done several times before her. Obviously the notion of weirdness was a big thing in their family. "These French!"

Two desires were vying for control of Sonya's mind. To find out more about this exciting man's life on the screens of France, or to try and fathom what on earth he was doing with Mary.

Her contempt for her sister and the need to elucidate the impenetrable mystery of how she had snailishly crawled her way into the life of this gorgeous movie star easily got the upper hand.

"What are you doing with my ugly stupid cow of a sister?" asked Sonya unceremoniously.

"That's not a very nice way to describe her," said Will, not feigning but genuinely shocked by this crude denigration of his girlfriend of an evening. "Not at all."

"Don't worry, I'm sure that she says far more wicked things about me, doesn't she?"

Will immediately seized this unexpected opportunity to play the diplomat, the broker of peace between these two women.

"Not at all! Quite the contrary!" he protested hotly. "She's been very complimentary indeed about your qualities, has hardly stopped talking about how much she admires you."

Sonya's jaw froze for a moment. "You're having me on, Charles, aren't you?"

Will warmed to the subject.

"Are you joking? Mary finds you beautiful, intelligent, generous, kind … She only regrets that you can be very rough with *her*. She sometimes even weeps about it. I wouldn't be at all surprised if your attitude towards her was not one of the reasons why she has—well what should we say?—rather let herself go physically in recent times."

Sonya looked momentarily stunned; Will decided to play with his advantage.

"I really do think that she loves and admires you very much. If I might be so bold as to say so, I suspect that you are perhaps both the victims of a misunderstanding. Perhaps it arose when you were adolescents, each trying to consolidate her ego in the shadow of the other, rivals for the attention of males, blaming your failures and problems on one another, believing the other to be your nemesis. But you should have put that all behind you a long time ago. I am sure that you could be great friends!"

It's a pity Herr Strumpf wasn't here to hear all that; he would have been proud of me, thought Will.

Word had soon gone like wildfire around the apartment about the presence of this French film star in their midst.

Will observed people getting a little closer to stare and smile at him.

One of them had been particularly unimpressed. Sonya's husband. Alerted perhaps by women's titters and whispering, he had kept his eye on the canapé and did not at all like to see his wife practically in the lap of this Alain Delon, or whoever he was. He arrived on the double and dragged her reluctantly off to dance with him. Her parting, whispered words, as she was whisked off to the dance floor in an adjoining room, were simply, "I still think she's an ugly stupid cow."

Now that a rumor had turned into a fact, Will was greeted with smiles and the odd "bonsoir," or even a couple of "Ça va?" as he moved around the room and took a few tidbits from the buffet. He could have sworn one of the petits fours contained a snail; perhaps his idea had not been so stupid after all?

Eventually, he decided to rejoin his employer. Perhaps she needed him.

"How are things going, Mary?" The trapped man was still in the corner with her.

"Wonderfully, thank you darling. Harold, this is my boyfriend Charles."

Mary's prey suddenly looked happier and took this as his moment to escape. He ducked under Mary's arm, which had been fixed on the wall beside him, laughed and was off, saying gaily, "I'm sure you'll want to be together a little."

"Shit," Mary told Will without further explanation, though she quickly regained her composure.

"So, you have met the evil Sonya. People have been saying that she practically ate you alive. What did she say about *me*? Or is it too vile to repeat?"

"She was very nice, actually. She thinks that you per-haps misunderstand her and have erroneously con-cluded that she doesn't like you."

"Erroneously my arse."

"No, no. I really do think that both of you are still living out old antipathies which should long ago have disappeared. She loves and admires the woman that you have become; she was especially impressed, if you don't mind me saying so, that you had caught *me* in your net. 'Net', that's exactly the word she used, just like you. You come from a family of fishermen, perhaps?" joked Will.

"Fish my arse," said Mary. "Let's go and dance."

She led him by the hand into the adjoining room. They jigged around to a pop song in the senseless, un-gainly way that two generations, at least, of young peo-ple had substituted for dancing in our time. At one moment, she grabbed his arm, pulled him towards her, and shouted above the music: "Did she really say that she admires me?"

Overwhelmed with desire for peace on earth and harmony between men, and sisters too, Will lied with great warmth and conviction:

"Absolutely! She adores and practically idolizes you."

Mary smiled whimsically and engaged with even more enthusiasm than before in the pantomime dance of arm thrusting and meaningless foot movements.

"You're a good man, Will," she bellowed above the

racket. "A good man or a bloody good liar, we shall see."

These qualities are not incompatible, thought Will. Nine months with Extra! had proved that to him beyond doubt or discussion.

CHAPTER SEVEN

"Stand back so I can take a better look at you."

"It's rather ill-fitting, isn't it? I could practically invite a friend inside," said Will, jerking both sides of the jacket open and shut like an exhibitionist.

"Beggars can't be choosers," Janet retorted tartly.

So, from hired hand I have become a beggar, thought Will. The lady's not particularly picky with her words.

Janet also felt that she had perhaps been uncharitable, and to cover her tracks brought Polonius to her rescue: "*Costly thy habit as thy purse can buy, but not expressed in fancy; rich, not gaudy; for the apparel oft proclaims the man.*"

The old fool's words did little to improve matters.

It certainly proclaims me, thought Will, no doubts there. He didn't own a single decent suit, let alone the black one appropriate for a funeral. It would be the first time he had worn another man's clothes. Except on the stage; and there they belonged to no one.

"It'll have to do," said Janet. "If you have time you could get it pulled in, I suppose. I wouldn't have a clue how to do that; sorry."

"Or perhaps I could add an extra row of buttons here to the left and pretend it's double-breasted?" he proposed.

"Very unlikely. Very impractical, I should say. It'll

have to do," she repeated. "Just manage as you can; a funeral isn't a beauty contest, after all."

Will wondered if Mrs Chapman ever looked anything other than beautiful. She was again, as on his first visit, dressed so elegantly it had made him blush to catch his own scruffy image in the entrance hall mirror. He knew nothing about fashion, but imagined her clothes came from only the top couturiers. Today, she floated about the salon in an ivory silk dress which embraced so lovingly her silhouette that he was forced to stare most of the time at her shoes for fear of having unbusinesslike and possibly even immoral thoughts.

"Are you married, Will?" asked Janet.

"No, no," laughed Will for no fathomable reason.

"A girlfriend?"

"Dozens of them, actually."

"Really? You naughty boy! You philanderer! *I will find you twenty lascivious turtles, ere one chaste man.* What do you suppose Shakespeare knew about the sex life of turtles? Odd statement, now I think about it."

Why did she call him 'boy', though? Mike called him 'boy', too, as well as 'my son'. Neither of them was the first to do it. She couldn't be a day over forty; Mike was twenty-five; other people more or less of his age did the same thing. Perhaps I should have a session with Strumpf about it?

"No, I was joking," said Will. "One of the 'lines'—as Mike puts it—of the Extra! agency is the boyfriend. I'm getting a lot of those jobs for some reason."

"So, you're a gigolo as well as a mourner?" asked

Janet with passionate, though disinterested, curiosity.

"Not at all. I thought the same thing when I was first interviewed; but it's a lot less exciting, more prosaic than that."

Without a word, Janet left the salon and, though it was only ten thirty in the morning, returned with a large scotch and a huge gin and tonic. She put the drinks down on the table between them, drew up her chair and urged him enthusiastically: "Go on!"

Will told her about the jilted and hideous girls and their desire to defend honor and avoid disgrace by showing off bogus men friends to their families and friends.

Janet did not mock these girls, as he expected her to do. She said rather: "I understand, I really do understand."

"But you, being so attractive, never had such a problem, surely?" Will blurted innocently.

Ignoring his rather forward remark, Janet replied, a little nostalgically: "Only since I got married—a bloody long time ago, in other words. How on earth does one reconcile the need to be desired and admired while dragging a miserable husband around, one who's jealous to boot? No, it's hopeless. I shall never do it again. Only flings with French dandies for me now! To hell with marital cosiness!"

Will had returned not only for the suit, but because Janet had proposed another briefing session about the man she wished she had made dive off the Matterhorn.

"Fred is in his late thirties, so you'll pull that off—

your Mike *did* listen carefully there. They met at Oxford; both studied physics and philosophy, which I am told are related, I can't imagine why. Do you know anything about either?"

"About physics, nothing whatsoever. I guess I could bluff my way through a conversation on philosophy, though."

"It really doesn't matter. Nothing either of them did after university had anything to do with one or the other as far as I know. And one easily forgets all that stuff. Anyhow, Ronald went into investment banking —that's where all this came from," she waved her extended arm casually around the room and the house beyond. "Fred went into the military. I made him a colonel. Actually, I said he was the youngest colonel in the British Army. I really don't know why I gave such stupid detail, but I like people to succeed; so why not Fred too?"

Will stood up, clicked his heels smartly together, raised his chin, saluted, and barked "The bathroom, please, Ma'am!"

A suicidal, jilted, Alpine-climbing cuckolded colonel stared at himself in the mirror. "Right, got that," said Will in a clipped, martial tone. "What else, I wonder?"

Their drinks had magically been refreshed when he returned to the salon. I thought I could put it away, Will reflected, but I've got nothing on this lady. Still, it's all part of the job.

"Let's talk about the photos," said Janet.

"The photos?"

"I need to get you into some of these pictures," she replied, waving at the walls and cabinets.

"How on earth can we do that?"

"It's called photoshop, or something. Stalin had it, if you remember. His friends disappeared one by one from his pictures when they fell out of favor. But you, Fred, are going to drop *in*. I've already identified a small business nearby where they can do that kind of thing. So, be a good boy, and send me a selection as quickly as possible so they can work on it. And then we can have you fishing with Ronald, or playing tennis with him, or attending our marriage—I didn't know any of my friends at that time and my family certainly wouldn't remember who was there."

Well, she was very thorough, that he could say.

Will agreed to sort through his photographs and to send her a collection from the last ten or fifteen years. What a curious story, he thought.

"Another thing, by the way: I have the green light from the coroner's office to fix a date and make arrangements for the burial. I don't know why it took them so long, but they have signed off on Ronald, finally. He did die of a heart attack, which is as we all suspected, brought on by an overdose of pills; they didn't yet say what kind, but we know, of course. Apparently, the coroner wants a meeting with me one of these days—he said even after the funeral, if that suited me—but in the meantime we can get on with the job. I was thinking of next Sunday; not too much traffic around the cemetery. That's in four days' time, so we can still meet a couple of times to get our stories accorded. I hope the annals of Ronald Chapman are proving useful to you?"

It sounded an awful lot like *anals* when she said it, but he dismissed the thought. She could be cruel, yes, certainly, but never vulgar, thought Will.

"No, I've not yet had a chance to dip into them," lied Will. "I shall soon, though." He couldn't possibly tell her for the moment what he had seen; none of it made any sense that he might usefully convey.

"In any case, I do not want to hear a word about them," said Janet with passion. "Even less if there is anything at all in them about *me*, which I very much doubt. Burn after reading!"

Janet had one last thought before conducting him to the street: "If you could bring a friend or two to the funeral, that would be splendid. They can come to the party afterwards, of course. I think that we're going to be a bit thin on the ground and that wouldn't look good at all. But no Chinese strippers."

"Oh, so Mike told you about *them*!" laughed Will.

"Yes, indeed. I didn't think it very appropriate, frankly, faced with a grieving widow, but he clearly couldn't help himself; he seemed so excited about the idea."

"I think he was just floating a balloon. He likes getting people's reactions."

And with that, Will headed to the underground. Tonight he was back to the bar, and tomorrow he had given himself the day off.

CHAPTER EIGHT

"**H**err Professor Doctor Doctor Doctor Doctor
Strumpf! Glad to see you!"

"Mutual. Gut efening, Vill."

"How's the mind business these days?"

"Not zo gut."

"I'm sorry to hear that. What's the problem?"

By professional habit, perhaps, Doctor Strumpf cast
a loving eye at the couch opposite the bar, but thought
twice about lying down and instead ordered his usual
slivovitz. Will kept at least two bottles of the brandy in
stock, for Strumpf, of course, but also the occasional
passing Croatian.

"Vell, I sometimes vonder if it's not over for us, ze
old schule. Ve had a gut hundred years, after all," said
Strumpf sadly. "Now, instead of coming to see me, zey
all go fishing in ze Amazon."

"Fishing in the Amazon? How extraordinary. Is that
some kind of new therapy?"

"Any of zose dee-li-cious black ladies bin in
tonight?" asked Strumpf distractedly. He loved joking
around with these lasses, even though he was never
quite sure of their status.

"No, no, they come in very late, you know, well
after midnight."

With no prospect of delicious black ladies in sight,
Herr Strumpf turned back to Will's question.

"Ze Amazon, you know, computers and all zat. Zey all buy books raazer zan come to consult doctors like me. Ze nin-com-poops, as you English call zem so beautifully. You know vy?"

"No," said Will.

"It's zese Americans. Zay haf finally discovered sinking! Und zay can't stop vriting about it. Everyvon should stop vot zey doing—und start to sink! 'Mind-*fool*ness', Ha! 'Meditation', Ha! Ze 'Emo*zio-naal* intelligence', Ha! Vot a stupid contradiction, hein? Five hundred years after Columbus, zay haf started to sink! Ha! Gott im Himmel!"

Herr Strumpf shuddered in visible distress, if not disgust, at the very idea that the Americans had begun to think and took another large gulp of slivovitz.

"There are certainly fortunes to be made though," said Will to cheer him up. "The mind is the new California! Most people are still very wobbly in that department and need all the help they can get. Perhaps you could bring these new ideas to England?"

"Zey are already here, Vill, already here, don't you vorry about zat! I sink zey vill not go so far, however. If zer is von zing ze Eenglish really hate, it is sinking!"

"I don't know," said Will, thinking that he should perhaps defend his countrymen's ardour for intellectual investigation.

Strumpf was in a particularly depressed and argumentative mood and pressed the issue.

"Zo, remind me of ze leading Eenglish philosopher of our day?"

"Off hand, I can't think of one, it's true."

"Not von? OK, my friend Vill, name two from ze 'hole tventieth century."

"Well, not many are household names, for sure. I know — Bertrand Russell!"

"Very gut, Vill. And ze second?"

"Um. Um … Yes—Ludwig Wittgenstein!"

"Ha. Haha! Hahaha! Lud-wig Witt-gen-stein," Strumpf drawled languidly. "Is very Eenglish name, ja? No, my friend, Wittgenstein vas from my country! Very un'appy man, very typically Austrian! It vas not an accident zat my profession vas born in Vienna you know. Very un'appy people! Do you know zat zhree of Ludwig's brozers zey killed zemselves? Zhree! And zat he often had ze same idea?"

"No, I can't say I did. Why would they do that?"

"My diagnozis is zat zey all suffered from self-disgust. Eet is very common vere I come from, it's our spezialität. Zom people turn it on zemselves and zom - ve haf a famous case I vill not mention—turn it against ze whole vorld."

Strumpf indicated his glass and Will topped it up.

"No, ze Eenglish ver not born to sink. Zey do not take zemselves seriously enuff for zat, not like zese Yankee doodles. I tell you, ze Eenglish are a people in search of mediocrity in zis matter of intellect. And not only zat! But I like zem for zis. A mediocre people is an 'appy people, I always zay."

"I wouldn't say that too loudly around here," advised Will kindly. "Not everyone will take it in the friendly

81

and helpful spirit you intend. They might very well suggest that you should do unspeakable things to yourself, before returning from whence you came, of course."

Happily, the bar was deserted save for another regular, a New Zealander on his sixth beer fighting a losing battle to keep his eyelids apart with the hand that did not grip his glass. He had been doing his best to follow the conversation and chipped in to repeat Strumpf's last words.

"A people in search of mediocrity? Hahaha! That's a good one, mate. But the English should count themselves lucky — in New Zealand, we found it!"

"Does any nation gain favor in your eyes?" Will asked Strumpf hopefully.

"Zose beautiful black ladies—vere are zey from again?"

"Nigeria, I think."

"Vell, zen I love Nigeria! Zey are so free, so musikaal, so happy, so funny, so friendly. Yes, ven I finally retire, I shall go and live in Nigeria! I am qvite sure zat zey need no psychoanalysts zere and zat zey vud laf zere heads off if you tried to sell zem zis mindfoolness business."

"Would you mind doing a great favor for me, Doctor?"

"A pleasure, I'm sure."

"Would you come to a funeral with me on Sunday? A close friend died and I frankly need the company."

"Vill, it vould be a great honor for me!" said Strumpf.

"Gif me ze details ven I come in tomorrow."

And at that, Doctor Strumpf descended unsteadily from his barstool, paid his bill, bid Will and his new New Zealand friend farewell and disappeared into the dank Islington night.

CHAPTER NINE

Will sometimes suspected that he lacked imagination and, quite possibly, ambition.

All around him, people seemed lost in extravagant fantasies: A Viennese shrink dreamed about a new life under the African sun among laughing black beauties; a former detective pondered how he might get Chinese strippers into London cemeteries without drawing the attention of the police; his receptionist, meanwhile, auditioned every passing male in a vain search for her Marlon Brando; a newly-widowed beauty planned to conquer the popinjays of France and Navarra as soon as she could get her husband buried; a fat girl called Mary walked the streets of the city hoping to be wrestled to the ground by a groper with whom she might fall in love.

And what do I dream about? Will asked himself. He could not think of anything that he wanted that he did not already possess. His life was simple and he loved it that way; he could not even imagine what any other life might be like to live. As long as he had a roof over his head and could afford food for his table and was in good health he was a happy man.

Will had few friends; indeed, it would be more accurate to say he had none at all, if he troubled to go through the ranks of his acquaintances in order to count them. He had rarely if ever given it any thought. Except now he had been forced to. Mrs Chapman had urged him to bring a 'friend or two' to Ronald's funeral, and only Strumpf had come to mind.

There were more than enough people in Will's life. He enjoyed very much the company of those with whom he shared long evenings in the bar as he served them; his acting work, such that it was, brought him together for brief periods with the most entertaining groups of truly delightful folk; his missions as an Extra! operative had taken him into new homes and unfamiliar social spheres. Everywhere, he felt comfortable and confident, and his desire to be with other people was perfectly satisfied by all these encounters. What more could friendships bring?

Girlfriends came and went in his life, of course. 'Real' ones, that is. In truth, they often went more rapidly than they came. And the speed of their departures had accelerated since he had become a man for hire. There had only been a handful since he joined Extra!, but when they discovered that he was renting himself out to other women they all took umbrage. One had even thought fit to threaten him: "It's them or me!" He had known her for precisely three days. Such instant possessiveness had left him shaking his head in wonder.

Love as sung by the poets since time immemorial seemed indeed to have passed Will by. He did not ache to taste its fruits, any more than he suffered to be friendless. He just thought it curious that he did not have these relationships that others fought and died for.

Will finished the coffee over which he had been having these reflections and cleared away the remains of his breakfast. He needed the table, otherwise he would probably not have bothered. He brought Mrs Chapman's brown suitcase out from under his bed, opened it up and examined its contents. There were two dozen or so notebooks, numbered on the inside covers, but none of them, apparently, dated.

He had read the first pages of the first of them the night he returned from Mary's party, but as yet had gone no further. This is where he had told a small lie to Ronald's widow. He thought it pointless to try and draw any conclusions from any of these unconnected sentences. And she still insisted that she did not want to know anything anyhow.

Will sat down, lit a cigarette and began to read again from the beginning. A citation headed the first page:

"What Diogenes was looking for with his lantern was an <u>indifferent</u> man." Cioran

Ronald had scribbled underneath, perhaps at a later date, since the words had been clumsily squeezed in before the first entry:

It was not I he found, alas.

The notebook contained little else than single sentences. Will read the first few:

In love, no half measures; joy or misery, nothing in between.

This furious passion for life cannot be contained, only broken or lost in madness.

Opposites attract. Hah! But the lamb cannot dwell with the wolf, whatever they say, even with a she-wolf in lamb's clothing and a lamb that everyone takes for a wolf.

It matters little if a man be false, as long as he knows where lies the truth.

Will flicked forward a few pages. There were hundreds of observations of this kind, not all complete nor all comprehensible, to him at least. Most had clearly been crafted by Ronald himself; these seemed less and less to reflect any desire to be pithy or literary as the pages went on; others were copied from books he was reading and the authors' names noted alongside them. He read a few more of Ronald's own thoughts, arbitrarily.

To silence a man by your indifference to the questions on which his life may hang merely by a thread is cruel beyond the imaginable.

To listen is a poor substitute indeed for the will to hear.

After reading Camus: Could the absurd standpoint imply as much power as sterility? Only boredom and indifference seem to stand in the way.

Push on, don't look back—don't even look forward, if you can help it!

Chapter Nine

Think of many things — dwell not too long on any of them.

In the room the women come and go, talking of Michelangelo.

That one's Eliot, thought Will, not Ronald, though he had not noted it. In any case, I'm not learning very much here. Perhaps Mrs Chapman is mistaken in believing I might get to know her late husband better through these notebooks.

Who would expect Fred to have penetrated Ronald's mind anyhow? People don't go around distributing aphorisms among their friends. What man shares those intimate reflections on life that he enjoys with himself? He'd be an embarrassment. No, reckoned Will, one does not speak of such things. I must search further for a few facts. Ronald could not have kept up these abstract notions over so many volumes.

Will shut the first notebook, delved into the suitcase and took another. He was afraid of picking one of the last of them, one written towards Ronald's unhappy end, so made sure it was numbered well before the last. He now checked and found that there were twenty-three notebooks in all. This was the tenth. It began:

I was washing the dishes. She pushed me aside, took a plate that was drying on the rack, held it up to the light and said: "Ronald, this is filthy! You're useless. Give it up." And with that, slid it back into the water. I picked it out of the sink once more and, calmly, coldly, dropped it on the tiled floor, where it broke into a dozen pieces at her feet. "That should fix the problem," I told her.

Now, that's more like it, he thought. Life as they lived it. He read on.

We pay twice, doubly victims. Once for the anger and hurt we provoke by our need to be alone, to suffer alone, to push away the other; then a second time, in reproaches, in moral lectures, in distance, when the pendulum swings back and we need more than anything in the world the warmth of a human being. So, we wander around in the slow shuffle of the lonely, cursing our need for solitude. Yes, yes, we 'want' it thus, as we stand accused; we 'want' it like a man with broken legs 'wants' crutches.

They tell you that their love is eternal, that they will always stick with you, put up with anything. And then one fine day, quite suddenly, they realize that they have had enough of their martyrdom and don't want to pay the price any longer. Who can blame them?

This is the worst thing; when 'she' becomes 'they'; that is the final death knell. It's like your Muslim neighbor. When 'he' becomes 'they', it's all over. You can start to sharpen your knives.

"When once the truth is grasped that one's own personality is only a ridiculous and aimless masquerade of something hopelessly unknown, the attainment of serenity is not very far off." Joseph Conrad. Let's hope he was right.

It's self-pity you have to look out for, Ronald old chap.

The whole of life is enveloped in our every tear.

The plate-smashing scene was the only 'event' as such that Will could find about their marriage in the volume. Ronald had quickly returned to his philosophical musings, if you could call them that. He was certainly disabused with life, thought Will simply. How does a man get to this point? he wondered.

He read on a little more:

"Should Wenger stay?" "Should Wenger go?" "Who's Wenger?" I ask casually, to provoke them. "You don't know Arsène?" they snivel in disbelief. "Arsène Wenger, the manager of Arsenal." "Arsenal, Arsenal what?" Only Janet laughs, bless her. "Ignore Ronald," she said, "He's teasing you. He can't stand soccer." She's right. One more evening with those football-loving morons will likely kill me.

Why do I go? Why do I do so much in my life that I do not want to do? I cannot bear the bank any longer, my money-grubbing colleagues revolt me, this social life is barren of any sense at all.

Perhaps the courageous are those who dissimulate and pretend? This is the question that keeps me awake at night. Why not just join the dance? Do you think that you are somehow superior, Ronald? Do you think that you have discovered something that the others don't know? Perhaps you're a lot less clever than you think.

Maybe you are actually the only one who hasn't grasped the rules of the game.

I started to talk about Nietzsche at the dinner last night, to try and raise the level of the conversation a little. "Nietzsche? Who does he play for?" asks one of the idiot trio. "Bayern Munich," chips in another. Well, I can't blame them for their revenge, I suppose.

Why do we punish ourselves so much? Why do we do so much that we don't want to do? Or is it just me? This I cannot fathom. How many other people are simply going through the motions, out of habit or obligation or want of anything better? Is it because they believe that they are wrong and not the others? I cannot believe it. But I may be mistaken about this as about everything else.

I've decided to stop going to the dinners. I will tell Janet tomorrow. She will be devastated; her whole life revolves around these parties with her friends; but it's me or her. Everyone takes me for some kind of tough guy who knows and does only what he wants, but it's quite untrue.

Our marriage is slipping away from us. I wonder if Janet knows it. Surely, she has to. Soon I must take my leave, if she does not do so first.

But I have not yet exhausted the bounds of pretense. I do not yet grasp how it came to this and hope that writing here will bring me to an understanding that for the moment escapes me. For a long time I have blamed her.

Blamed her for failing to try and comprehend me. But how wrong that might be! I see more and more that when one is unhappy one must find someone to accuse. It is too much to take it upon oneself, and I have been no exception to this rule. But of one thing I am certain: it does not matter in the slightest! When it's over, it's over. There's no point at all in apportioning responsibility, in seeking who's to blame. What hell we go through for nothing.

Will closed the notebook and sighed. He needed to get outside, where the bright spring day beckoned him. He would go for a walk in the park and think of nothing at all. This was, after all, the day he had promised to take off from work.

The trees danced like South Sea maidens—now to the right, now to the left—in the swirling wind and glittering sunlight as he set off happily down the street.

CHAPTER TEN

"Good morning."

"Morning," echoed around the conference room.

"I've invited you here for a Marlon Brando impersonation contest."

They all laughed. Blanche, who was taking notes, stuck her tongue out at Mike.

"No. I've asked you in for two or three reasons. First of all, it's the first anniversary of the creation of Extra! When we're through here, I'm taking you all for a bloody good lunch, starving devils that you are, to celebrate with me and Blanche."

They all applauded.

"Secondly, and not least, I thought that you should finally meet each other. You are my A-Team, the Extra! elite—my biggest earners, if I can be crudely pecuniary."

"You've never hesitated up till now," joked one of the operatives.

Mike adored repartee, even aimed at himself, and stuck his thumb up.

"Thirdly, and in the same spirit, you're not going to get lunch for nothing, so I thought we could first have a little discussion, an ideas session, about the development of the agency's products and services. After all, what's good for me is good for you.

"First, though, introduce yourselves and tell us all a bit about your missions, your specialities. Will, you start."

"Thanks, Mike. I'm Will Power, alias Bob, Daniel, Eamonn, Peter, Paul, Mary—I jest—Patrick, George, Jack, Michael, Bela—I once played, rather poorly, a Hungarian—Richard, John, Albert, Charles, a few others I've forgotten. Right now, I'm Fred. I do boyfriends, job candidates, and will shortly be Extra!'s first mourner."

"Mourner? How's that?" asked a friendly fellow opposite him.

"It's our new line," Mike intervened proudly. "I hope so, at least. Will's going to weep over the grave of a man he never knew."

"I'm even going to give his eulogy," said Will. "I didn't have a chance to tell you."

"Interesting, very interesting," said Mike, instantly thinking about a special encomium supplement to the mourner tariff.

"Unfortunately, I have to write it myself."

I'll double that, thought Mike about the initial rate he had just created.

Another operative had instantly had the same thought and chimed in: "Isn't that a good avenue for development? Variable fees according to the extent of our engagement?"

"Can you give me another case where this might crop up, Peter, apart from writing and pronouncing eulogies?" asked Mike.

"I have one from last week, actually," said Peter. "I was barracking this politician at a public hearing about social housing, suggesting that he was talking rubbish about the lack of need or space for new homes in the borough, when he invited me to come up to the stage and share my wisdom, if I knew so much about the subject. Our client, who was lurking nearby, gave me the nod. I made a fifteen-minute speech of sheer genius, if I may say so. They couldn't shut me up … the council's moral obligations to provide affordable homes to the poor … the rise in the number of homeless in our streets … the children's lives ruined by the lack of a decent, secure environment, and so on. What I didn't know, I made up, of course, like we all do. I could have done some of the technical stuff too, but people want emotion. I had them weeping in the aisles—and turned the majority round in favor of the new housing project. The power of rhetoric is a sight to behold, my friends. I never cease to be amazed."

"The politician didn't stand a chance," laughed Mike. "Peter has a masters in sustainable cities. I picked it up on his CV in our data bank. That's why I sent him along."

"Who was the client?" asked another operative.

"A property developer," said Mike shamelessly.

"So," resumed Peter, "perhaps our contracts could stipulate that we must get additional payment for making speeches, or something like that."

"Fine idea," said Mike, "I'll work on it and let you all know."

Will wondered whether Mike would have taken on the job for a property developer who wanted social housing destroyed and replaced by luxury apartments. Probably, he thought. He had once told him: "Will, my boy, I don't make moral judgements, no way. I might as well change business if I did that. What's *legal* is my only concern. My moral compass is the law."

The man opposite Will couldn't get the mourner out of his mind and chimed in again: "Could you tell us the funeral story, Will? I can't imagine what that's about."

Will looked at Mike, who nodded and said: "Make it short."

"Well, it's complicated. And getting more so each day. This woman, our client, invented a friend for her husband when he refused to go out with her any longer. He was a cover; she pretended he was with him so she didn't have to make up excuses for her own friends each time. She told them that her husband's friend was going through a marriage break up and needed his support. He even tried to kill himself, between climbing mountains. Then the husband himself committed suicide, leaving the woman with a fictitious friend on her hands. Everyone demands now to meet him and he has to play a star role at the funeral. I'm reading the husband's diaries in preparation, but there's obviously nothing in them about the friend. Because he doesn't exist, of course, or didn't until Extra! stepped in. Is that clear?"

"As clear as mud," said Mike. "Thanks, Will. You

may like to work a little on the eulogy, though ... Frank, introduce yourself."

"Thanks, Mike. Frank Ormrod. Pleased to meet you all. Like all of us, I guess, I do boyfriends, companions, but also now a couple of husbands."

"Tell us about one of the husband missions," said the insatiably curious operative who had asked for the funeral story. He was quite new on the books and wanted to know more about what he was getting himself into.

Mike nodded again.

"Fine. This was just last week. It's not a tale for children, though, so please put your hands over your ears if you're sensitive," he joked.

"Our client was a young, married woman having an affair, who wanted to break up with her lover and go back to her husband. A touching story, I think you will agree. Well, she just couldn't find the courage to tell this paramour that it was all over and that he was now toast. And perhaps more importantly, she feared that her husband might find out what she had been up to; that the lover might take his revenge for being cast off, for example, and expose her infidelity, ruining her plans to resume happily married life.

"So this clever and duplicitous woman—you have to admire her imagination—dreams up the idea of being exposed to a *fake* husband from Extra! so that there is nothing that this man can reveal to anyone, of course. She invites loverboy over one afternoon while her real husband is away on a business trip, gives me a set of spare keys to the house and at the agreed time I burst in on them. In flagrante delicto, actually. She could really have spared me that, but I guess she couldn't resist a last fling.

"You can imagine the scene: outraged husband screaming that his wife is a whore, that he has been betrayed, that if loverboy doesn't get out immediately he cannot guarantee his physical integrity—in plain English, 'I shall smash your face in and cut off your ...'"

"Yes, yes," Mike interrupted, "we get the general idea."

Everyone laughed.

"Anyhow, I didn't even let the poor bastard put his trousers and shirt back on and he scarpered half-naked off out of the house and down the street. Mission accomplished. Extra! at your service."

"Don't you think it was all a bit dangerous?" asked another operative. "Supposing he had put up a fight, attacked you?"

"I thought about all that beforehand, of course," Mike reassured the meeting. "Never would I put any of you in any kind of danger," he said solemnly. "But no, lovers don't attack husbands, never, ever. That would be the world on its head. There's still a bit of morality left in this country, you know," he said confidently.

The meeting went on for another hour or so. Each of the operatives searched for the best and most mysterious stories to regale his colleagues. Then Mike, well pleased about the gathering, wound things up.

"I've enjoyed this discussion very much. I hope

you're pleased to finally meet some of the other failed actors who work for me as you do."

They all laughed. Nothing that this Mike could say could offend them. He was spontaneous and lovable and truly kind, and he could personally take it on the chin even better than the next man. That they all knew.

Will nevertheless saw fit to add, as an afterthought: "On the stage of life, Mike, you have got the best."

"Quite, quite," said Mike. "I'm very proud of all of you. And now for the great lunch that I promised. We'll get a chance to continue this conversation at table and over a drink or six. Follow me. The place is just around the corner."

They all trooped out after the boss and walked to the restaurant where Mike had hired a private room.

Drinks finally in hand, the operatives soon cornered Blanche and started murmuring to her and each other.

Three waiters watched them and listened discretely. They heard strange hissing and shushing sounds as the men stuck out their jaws, pursed their lips and mumbled incomprehensibly between their teeth.

The waiters looked at each other and whispered.

One said: "A dentists convention?"

Another: "Perhaps they're ventriloquists?"

The third: "No, I think it's an outing from the loony bin. Let's be careful lads."

Whatever the waiters thought, Blanche remained unfulfilled. Not a decent Brando among them, she protested; no one could say her name like Marlon and they might as well just give up trying.

CHAPTER ELEVEN

Janet called Will again the next day.

"Will, all these funeral arrangements I have to make are getting completely out of hand. I don't want to involve anyone else at all at the moment; would you mind very much helping me?"

"Of course, Mrs Chapman, I'd be happy to. What can I do?"

Will had already cleared with Mike that he could continue working until the funeral at least; then they would review the contract again. "Let it run, boy, let it run," the boss had laughed. "The meter's ticking along very nicely."

Before anything else at all, Mrs Chapman wanted him to contact Ronald's bank and "tell them that he won't be returning to work."

"They don't know he's dead?"

"No, I never got round to informing them. In any case, he was enjoying a few days off when he died, before he died, that is, so they probably wouldn't have missed him yet. But most importantly, I want you to invite his closest colleagues to the funeral, whoever they are. He loathed them all, or so he told me, but it's very important for show, particularly for the family, that some of them should be there."

Janet gave him a number for the bank and the name of Ronald's superior. She also asked whether he would go to her florist and order a first-class wreath, the most expensive they could put together. She was sure that he had good taste in flowers and would pick a very fine composition.

"What words would you like on the ribbon?"

"I have absolutely no idea. Find something appropriate on the Internet and call me back, would you?"

So, first job the bank. A Mr Samuels. Will called and was informed that the man was unavailable; instead he was put through to a colleague.

"Good morning. My name is Colonel Acton. I'm calling on behalf of Mrs Janet Chapman. I have some bad news, I'm afraid. Her husband Ronald is dead, the heart."

"Good Lord, I'm sorry," said the man sympathetically. "But why didn't anyone tell us before?"

"Mrs Chapman apologizes for that, but she's been very busy, as you will understand."

"Even so, five months …"

"I beg your pardon? Five months of what?" enquired Will.

"Since he disappeared."

"No, he died a week ago, actually," Will clarified, puzzled by the man's comments.

"He had been ill, then? A real pity no one told us," he repeated.

"I'm sorry, I don't really get the drift. It was sudden, a heart attack. What do you mean by five months?"

"We haven't seen him since … November, I think it was. Didn't you know he had stopped coming to the bank? We tried calling him a few times, but never got an answer. We never suspected for an instant that he had died."

"Yes … yes … I understand," said Will haltingly, though he didn't. "But he only died last week …"

"Good Lord," said the man again. "We thought he had gone AWOL, as it were. Just between you and me, we have a fair few colleagues over time who crack and hop it. Burn-out or something like that. There's a lot of pressure in this business, you know, bloody markets going up and down like yoyos."

"I understand. But since he *is* dead, Mrs Chapman asked me to invite Ronald's closest colleagues to his funeral. Could you do that for him, for her?"

"Yes, of course, of course, I'll round up a couple of the lads for sure. Can you send me details by mail? Time and place and where we should have a wreath delivered?"

Will promised to send the information, then saw fit to add: "To be very frank with you and in complete confidence, Mrs Chapman wasn't aware that Ronald wasn't going to the office as usual. So I would ask you to please not mention it when you see her."

"No problem," said the man kindly.

Well, well, well, thought Will after finishing the call. What an earth was going on? He would have to go back to Ronald's diaries, that was sure. Perhaps there was a clue there?

In the meantime, he had to fix the wreath, which meant going to Janet's florist in Chelsea. First, though, he must find the words for the ribbon; one couldn't improvise these things.

Will found an appropriate Internet site, as Janet had instructed, and a list of suggestions. He called her.

"Mrs Chapman, I've fixed the bank, they promised to round up a few colleagues, and I've given them the details."

"You're a darling, Will."

'Darling'? Though the word meant nothing, he felt a flush of warmth sear through his body.

"For the wreath, I've found a list of potential phrases. Could I read them to you?"

"Go ahead."

"'I know how you are feeling'."

Janet said nothing.

"'It's for the best'."

"Will my boy, I think you're on the wrong page. These are things one might say to the defunct's relatives, not parting messages for *him*!"

"You're right. Sorry. Hold on a second. Got it. Do any of these please you? 'To me you were so special. Someone good and true. Never will I forget you, I thought the world of you'."

Will thought he heard a snigger on the line, but in the absence of any comment, he went on: "'Death may leave a heartache no one can heal, but love leaves a memory that no one can steal'."

Still, Janet said nothing, though he heard a muffled choking sound.

"I'll go on: 'Many friends come into our lives, but only a few leave with their footprints on our hearts'."

This time, Janet exploded with frank, hysterical laughter.

"My God, Will, that's so, so, so funny. You're making these up, aren't you? 'A footprint on my heart'? Hahaha! Well, he certainly trampled on all that I hold dear, if that's what that means."

"Sorry, Mrs Chapman, I didn't invent these, you know, they're right here. In any case, you would need a two-yard wide wreath for a ribbon that could take all that. Here, I've found a couple of shorter sentiments. 'Always in my heart'? ... 'Gone but never forgotten'?... 'In loving memory'? ... 'Till we meet again'?"

"I bloody well hope not!" Janet interrupted.

"But Will, enough fun and laughs. I've got it: Just 'Rest in Peace, Janet'. It doesn't commit me to any lie, and I would sincerely want that for him, however meaningless the words may be when you think about them."

She thanked him again and said she must get on with her invitations, with tying up details with the Plums, and with the wake plans.

"One last thing, Will. I'm sorry, but you have to come here on Saturday and meet my mother. She's staying with me for the night and insists without discussion that she must meet you. On Sunday, there won't be time; she has to rush off just after the lunch. Is that OK?"

Will said he would have to cancel his shift at the bar that evening, but that if she didn't hear from him again she should consider it done.

Janet went about her business and he went to the florist. He would have liked to solve the bank mystery as soon as possible, but it might have to wait until after the funeral. He would have to trust Ronald's colleagues to keep quiet until then as they had promised to do.

CHAPTER TWELVE

"He was a good man, Ronald."

"I know, mother, I know very well."

"Why did he kill himself?"

"Would you like a drink?" Janet asked her, leaving the salon and the question suspended in the air.

"A sherry, please, dear."

Janet had been dreading this confrontation with her mother, who had barely arrived from the station and installed herself in an armchair. She looked at the kitchen clock and silently urged Will to hurry up and join them, to share the interrogation and deflect some of the attention from her. She took as long as possible to prepare their drinks, but still he did not come. She even threw down a gin and tonic right there and then and appeared back in the salon carrying her second glass.

"I was asking why you think Ronald killed himself," her mother resumed.

"Yes, I know. Do we *have* to talk about it right now?" At any time, in fact, she thought but didn't say.

"It's our only chance, my dear. You are always so evasive on the telephone and tell me nothing."

"What do you know about our relations these past months, this past year or so? I know you two were as thick as thieves, always jabbering away secretly together."

"There was nothing secret between us, Janet, don't exaggerate. He was just kind and attentive and actually wanted to hear about my life, particularly since your father's death. He wanted to know how I was getting on, whether I was lonely, what I was reading, and so on. You didn't come up as often as that in our conversations. Quite the contrary."

Where could she start? Why *did* she think Ronald had finished it all? The truth was that she had decided to leave the question unanswered, perhaps never to return to it. Who knew?

"Only in newspapers and novels do people kill themselves for a clear-cut reason, mother, don't you think? I suppose he'd just had enough. You know how he struggled, how terribly, chronically bored with everything he had become, how he had lost his enthusiasm for all those things—fishing, riding, shooting, walking, partying, going to the theater and opera—which had once amused him. The man of action I married retreated into his study and I never saw him again. And then Fred showed up, of course." Christ, she had almost forgotten to put him in the story.

"Ah yes, the famous Colonel Acton. Is he coming?"

"Yes, mummy, he should be here any minute, just as you asked."

"And Ronald's work?" the question machine resumed.

"He had come to hate it. He used to come home full of pride, boasting about the deals he had done and the fortune he was building for us. But little by little he began cursing his fate to have 'ended up like T. S. Eliot', as he put it. In other words, in a bank. The only difference is that Ronald wasn't a poet. In the end he stopped talking about his work altogether and would ignore me when I asked him about his days at the office.

"Did I tell you that I got a job too, mummy?"

"Good Lord, no. I thought you were living happily off the fat of the land, as it were, shopping and endlessly reading your precious Shakespeare. What do you do?"

"I work for a publishing house, reviewing the odd manuscript, chatting with passing authors, making tea. I only took the job in the first place because an old school friend runs the place and asked whether I might help him out. I've been there for six months but will certainly give it up now."

"And what do you plan to do?"

"I think I'll go abroad," said Janet staring at the ceiling, as though this was where abroad was situated, and thinking about beaches, bistros, yachts and being served and quite possibly also seduced by tall, dark, handsome strangers.

Her mother took a modest sip of sherry; Janet gulped down a huge mouthful of gin; the interrogation continued. I shall fire that Will fellow, she screamed silently.

"So, he became a bit reclusive, shut himself away to think, but what about you two, your marriage?"

"We weren't happy together, to put it mildly. In fact, mother, I suspect that we perhaps were *never* happy as a couple."

"What do you mean that you *suspect* it," her mother retorted. "You either were happy or you weren't happy," she said coldly.

"No, I think you're wrong. It's never as cut and dried as that. Particularly with extroverts like me and Ronald, or rather the Ronald I thought I had married, the Ronald as he was until he started exploring the depths of his navel. These things are so ambiguous, mummy. I know it sounds silly, but I don't believe I ever asked myself what I thought about him; I never asked myself whether I was happy either. I'm not that kind of person. I was 'in love', of course, but I'm less and less sure that I was in love with him, whoever he was. And I was too busy having fun to examine my state of mind very much."

"What on earth do you mean 'whoever he was'?"

"Well what can I say? There's this image, this idea of marriage as some kind of extraordinarily secret place where two people share unspeakable intimacy and become profoundly knowledgeable about the other. I don't say that this is impossible, but I think it's very rare. Even today, I was reading in the newspaper about this man who was leading a total double life. He had two wives, two sets of children, in towns one hundred miles apart, and *three* mistresses scattered all over the countryside in between. He pretended to all of them that he was a top surgeon, called off day and night for emergency operations. In fact, he was nothing more than a serial fornicator living off an inheritance and doing no work as such at all. Can you imagine, mummy, for

twenty years he managed to fool two wives and count-
less other women with a totally bogus life. No one suspected anything at all, nothing, until he was killed in a
road crash and everything came out. What did *you* really know about daddy, for example? And what did he
know about you?"

"Get me another drink, would you, daughter?" her
mother said in place of a reply.

Janet complied readily; her own glass was begging
to be refilled also. On her way through the entrance
hall, she looked forlornly at the front door and muttered
"Where the hell are you, Colonel bloody Acton?!"

"But Janet," her mother resumed as she returned,
"what are you implying with this surgeon's disgraceful
story?"

"Only this, mummy: We really may know little or
nothing about the person to whom we are supposed to
be closest. We may not even be especially interested either, to tell the harsh truth that no one admits. After all,
when all is said and done, we don't even really know
ourselves for the most part. We just get on with life; we
don't sit around indulging in permanent introspection
and soul searching. If we did, we wouldn't do anything
at all. I think that's where Ronald took a wrong turn.
He started thinking too much, analysing everything
endlessly. No good can come of that."

There was silence again between them. Janet's
mother got up and wandered around the room examining the photographs of her dead son-in-law. At one

moment, Janet heard a restrained sob. She hadn't given up her questioning, though.

"Ronald told me that I was the only person who listened to him," said the older woman.

"That's completely unfair," replied Janet. "Completely untrue."

"He said that you dismissed his philosophical concerns; that you were not interested in his search for sense, for meaning in his life."

"I'm not Mrs bloody Schopenhauer, mother!"

"Don't swear, daughter, you know I don't like that."

"I didn't marry Ronald for seminars on metaphysics," Janet defended herself. "It wasn't a matter of discussing abstract concepts for fun, I don't mind that at all. But you have to understand that he became negative, cynical, considered simple, superficial conversation as 'mentally depraved'; that he fell into a downward spiral of death and destruction."

"Aren't you being a little dramatic?"

"No mother. It's most unfair," she repeated. "Everything became too difficult. He walked blindly into a cul-de-sac and couldn't find his way out again. He made such a fuss about *everything*. He wouldn't meet anyone, wouldn't go out in the evening, wouldn't even go for a walk in the park. We couldn't even go shopping in Harrods without him becoming hysterical and storming out after ten minutes to go and wait for me in a pub, shouting that everything was 'futile', even though he loved very much what I bought to eat, even though he never let the futility of food shopping ruin his appetite. He became totally unfit for even the simplest activities of a normal life."

Before Janet's mother could think of a rejoinder, the doorbell rang. Oh merciful God, thought Janet.

"About bloody time, Colonel Acton!" Janet whispered to Will in the hall.

"Sorry, Mrs Chapman, I'm really sorry. But I was struggling with the eulogy. How's it going?"

"The victims of the Spanish Inquisition got off more lightly."

Janet took him into the salon and presented him to her mother.

"Good evening, Mrs, Mrs ... Mrs Janet's mother."

"Good evening, Colonel. The name's Black, but please call me Irene."

"Thanks. I'm Fred."

"Scotch, Fred?" asked Janet.

"Indeed, that would be wonderful."

"It's very nice of you to come around," said Mrs Black. "Ronald did mention you a few times, though I had no idea that your friendship went back so long. I was just looking at your Oxford photograph."

"Yes, yes," said Will. "We went back a long way." He hadn't yet had a chance to see the pictures, so didn't know what she was talking about.

"But you know how it is in the army, these days, with all these conflicts in far-flung lands. Between Afghanistan and Iraq and a few rather less publicized engagements in the Middle East, we're kept pretty busy, and Ronald and I didn't get to spend a lot of time together, except in these past few months."

"What regiment are you in?" asked Mrs Black.

God, we didn't decide on that one, thought Will.

"You know something about the army then?" said the smiling colonel to play for time.

"Nothing at all."

"Special services, you know. The forces the public doesn't hear much about. All highly confidential and secretive."

"What's 'highly confidential'?" asked Janet gaily as she re-entered the salon with a tray of drinks and some sandwiches. Will's arrival had completely alleviated her anguish.

"He was talking about his secret life in the army," said Mrs Black. "Sounds very intriguing. He's probably one of those fellows who knocked off Gaddafi," she winked at her daughter. "Good riddance."

"Oh yes, Fred's a real hero," laughed Janet. "Youngest colonel in the British Army, I believe."

Never one to lose sight of her subject, Mrs Black dropped the military and began again about Ronald.

"Colonel—Fred, why do you think he decided to leave us?"

"First of all, Irene, I'd like to say that Ronald was a good man."

"He was, wasn't he?" she interrupted. "That's what I was saying to Janet."

"And I agreed," said Janet, tired beyond measure with the discussion.

"But he was very unhappy. Why? Well that's something between a man and himself. In a way, I like to think it's entirely to his credit. At some point, he stopped taking life at face value and began asking himself some of those profound questions about existence that we should all perhaps confront but that out of a lack of courage or honesty or ambition we avoid and relegate to another time—or perhaps never ask at all."

This is good, thought Janet. Keep it up, Will my boy.

"When I last came back from a long mission abroad, we decided to see more of each other. I had problems of my own, I must confess. But he was already long gone. The worm was not only in the fruit but had practically consumed it. He never said it quite this way, but I'm convinced that he had given up on life, his life, and that he couldn't find the way back, couldn't find any reason to reconstruct the foundations of an existence. He thought that everything was pointless, useless, vain, destroyed for ever; he had lost his taste for living, I can't think of any other way to say it."

Not only is that good, thought Janet, it's true, it was exactly so.

"What a waste, what a waste," said Mrs Black.

Little more was said, for there was little more to say. They ate their sandwiches in silence and each went off into his or her thoughts. Will wanted to get out as soon as possible to finish Ronald's eulogy; Janet wanted to get her mother to bed and never have to answer another question in her life; Mrs Black's thoughts wandered back to her own life as she belatedly asked herself what indeed she had really known about Janet's father. Soon, each realized that the evening had come to an end. Will pleaded the need to get home and resume his writing. The women readily agreed to let him go and indeed took his departure as a reason to cease also their exploration of Ronald's life and death. It had been very short, if awkward, all things considered. But a man is easily forgotten and done with, once he's out of it all.

As she showed him back into the night, Janet took Will's hand, squeezed it, and said: "You're a credit to the British Army, Acton. See you at the cemetery."

CHAPTER THIRTEEN

A black Fedora bobbed up and down behind the tombstones opposite Ronald's grave. Christ, thought Will, he couldn't keep away from Extra!'s first funeral job.

Janet had dispensed with the services of a priest. Ronald had been a staunch atheist, and she didn't want him rolling over in his grave, as it were, even before they had dropped him into it. For herself, she frankly didn't care one way or the other. She was grateful to the Church nevertheless; it was only recently that they had allowed suicides the right to grace their consecrated ground at all. She had skipped the chapel too, and they had swung through the gates of the cemetery and descended from their various cars directly on the little road leading to the plot she had chosen.

Shuffling into some kind of formation, the mourners solemnly followed the hearse the short distance from the cemetery entrance to Ronald's awaiting tomb, five abreast in five or six rows, the widow, her mother, Will and a couple of the pushier guests, those who must always be in the front of anything, in the first line.

Plum and Son, leading their hearse on foot, looked even more death-like and grim than usual, outdone only in their gravity, if this was possible, by their sinister assistants, who had clearly all been hired for their naturally lugubrious countenances. Janet wondered idly if the Plums ever laughed (she had no doubt about their employees, who would soon be mocking all of them over a beer in the local pub, she was sure). She simply couldn't imagine the Plums at a football match or a rock concert, or walking through the fields in the summer sunshine, or swimming happily in the sea, or, God forbid, making love. These men were made to be the mirror of grief, she thought, and that alone. There was, of course, always Sartre and his waiter to put a grain of doubt in her mind ...

Janet had long hesitated about what she might wear; *about what she might get away with*, actually. Yes, of course, black, that's what everyone did, that's what everyone expected. Black, black, black. But to hell with 'everyone', she had thought. Am I a free woman or not? Can I make my own decisions or not? Can I defy custom and expectations or not? She had decided that she could and would indeed. So she had chosen—bought, in fact—a purple Chanel suit with black and glittering silver trimmings and a rimless black pillbox hat. She had decided against a veil. She was not shutting herself away a minute longer, even though she would wear her best amber and gold-framed sunglasses to keep away the others' prying eyes. Examining herself in the mirror before leaving home that morning, she had found that she looked absolutely stunning; for some reason, images of Jackie at JFK's funeral floated through her mind. In any case, it was the perfect outfit to make the transition from death to renewed life, she thought.

The methodical Plums had set up a brass lectern near the head of the grave. This was where Will took his place as the other mourners clustered round the tomb and the funeral parlor staff extracted Ronald from their van and laid him by the side of the hole awaiting him.

Will already felt considerable emotion welling up in him as he surveyed the small crowd while Plum & Son made their preparations. Next to Mrs Chapman stood her mother; on the other side, her brother; other relatives placed themselves around and opposite them. Three very pretty women she had briefly introduced to Will as her closest girlfriends stood together at the foot of the grave, their men a little off to the back. Behind them, Herr Strumpf, wearing what looked to Will like tailcoat hand-me-downs from the Vienna Philharmonic, stared intently at his feet. The group was completed by four men who had made no effort at all to look like anything other than the impeccable, clean-shaven, manicured and perfumed City bankers they clearly could only be. Ronald's former—very former, as it turned out—colleagues. Mike had also come out of hiding, hat now in hand, and was timidly shuffling his way towards them, all the while trying to avoid Will's eyes.

The whole business should be as short as possible, Mrs Chapman had told Will. "Poetic, cultured, moving and short, very short," had been her exact words in giving him her instructions. She had said that he should earn his extravagant fee by composing Ronald's eulogy himself. She frankly didn't care what he recounted, as long as it raised no one's suspicions and, she repeated, was poetic, which was the most important thing of all.

As soon as everything was in place, Will cleared his throat and embarked on his speech:

> *"Your lost friends are not dead, but gone before, advanced a stage or two upon that road which you must travel in the steps they trod."*

> *I cite the words of Aristophanes, the Father of Comedy, whom Ronald and I loved so dearly. We studied his writings together at Oxford, and I recall with emotion the evenings of laughter and camaraderie we enjoyed together in his study or mine reading the dialogues from his plays. We were inspired to learn that Plato shared our love and that the works of Aristophanes were found under the great philosopher's death-bed pillow. If death had not struck down Ronald so suddenly, I like to think that he too would have chosen such words to accompany him on this journey …*

I didn't know that Ronald read Aristophanes, thought Janet, forgetting for a moment that Will was making it all up.

> *Yes, Ronald gave his working life to the noble profession of investment banking, to creating the wealth that every society needs to prosper. And we are very happy that today several of his closest bank colleagues have joined us to show their deep respect for his achievements in that business. But he was a human too …*

A few of the guests sniggered, and the bankers looked quizzically at each other.

... and found great joy when he left the City to go home to the books of philosophers, of poets, of writers, with whom he shared his evenings ...

Rather than me, thought Janet.

For our dear Ronald was a thinking man, a man devoted to finding a sense to his life, something which is perhaps a little too rare in our times ...

Come on, Will, don't moralize and lecture us, Janet said to herself. No one's interested in your thoughts about contemporary intellectual and spiritual life, that of Ronald or anybody else, come to that.

Indeed, in recent times we resumed with those evenings of our youth and met very often for recitations and to remind ourselves how right Aristophanes had been about the comedy of life.

Well, that covers me, thought Janet. You certainly get a few points there, Will my boy.

Will paused and looked around to see how his eulogy might be going down. He couldn't learn anything from Mrs Chapman through her sunglasses. He did remark that the three pretty women at the foot of the grave were weeping willfully.

As he glanced at the others, a raven appeared from nowhere, swooping down with a screech and landing among the white lilies on the top of Ronald's coffin. It immediately began rapping noisily on the oak wood.

This is most out of order, thought Plum the Elder, pained that such a spanner could be thrown into his well-oiled machinery. He contemplated the walking cane upon which he was leaning and thought to strike the bird.

In the embarrassed silence that came over the whole group, Janet suddenly spoke up, loud and clear: "*Tis some visitor ... tapping at my chamber door—only this and nothing more.*"

And in the spirit of Will's remarks, she looked around her and said softly: "Ronald loved Poe too. I'm sure that he would have appreciated this little visit. Fred?"

What a woman, thought Will, what a marvelous, wonderful woman. The raven had done the right thing and flown off. Will resumed:

> *I should not talk about myself on such an occasion. But what could better illustrate what a good man, what an excellent and loyal friend Ronald could be than to tell you what fantastic support he has been to me personally over the painful trials I have been through this past year or so. He was always there for me, always gave his time and love unstintingly, neglecting even many of his own obligations. For this I must thank him from the depths of my heart ...*

With rising, true emotion, Will rambled on in a similar vein for a few more minutes about Ronald's qualities and, with great tact and moderation, even added a few innocuous lies about the wonderful life he and Janet had shared and the depth of their love. He thought he saw her wince under her spectacles; he decided to wind things up:

> *As those closest to Ronald and Janet will know, they shared a passion for Shakespeare and theater in general. With what else could I thus end these remarks than a few words from the master: "Though death be poor, it ends a mortal woe."*

Goodbye, dear Ronald, rest in peace.

Very good, thought Janet, very satisfying. It was one of the Richard's—most certainly—II or III, she couldn't recall. She would have to look it up later; for once her memory failed her.

At the nod of her head, the Plums sprang into action and the burial took its normal course.

Will had begun sobbing, truly and deeply moved by his own rhetoric and the occasion. It was never banal when a man died; it was always a tragedy.

Other guests hesitated whether or not to throw earth on the descending coffin, but seeing that Janet hadn't done this, restrained themselves.

Everything then passed in the most perfect silence. Only a few ravens could be heard laughing in a nearby tree.

※

Setting off quickly out of the cemetery, Janet left her mother's side and linked her arm with Will's. She said no word, but looked up at the bright sun that had broken through the clouds and bathed her face in its glow and warmth.

Ronald's colleagues rapidly paid their respects to her and bolted to wherever bankers spend their Sunday afternoons.

Plum the Elder bowed with great dignity and apparent sorrow before Mrs Chapman, then slipped into the passenger seat of his hearse and commanded his son to drive slowly away.

Sheila, Veronica and Sally trotted arm in arm towards the exit, also silent, their eyes not yet emptied of their tears, followed by their gossiping husbands.

The Chapman family at large lingered and chatted, anxious to catch up with news of each other's lives. They didn't see each other very often.

Herr Strumpf was in quite a state. "Vot a tragedy, vot a tragedy," he murmured to himself, tears cascading down his old cheeks. "So young, so young. So sad. He could have been my son." He cried for himself and for the too-rapid passage of time.

Will saw the weeping Professor, excused himself to Janet, walked back and took Strumpf by the hand. "Let's go and have a few drinks," he proposed to console the dear old man. Strumpf, his head bowed in embarrassment for his emotion, said simply: "Ja, ja, ja." Will guided him towards one of the awaiting cars.

Only one person was left. Mike. He hung timidly behind Strumpf, his Fedora back on his head. Will shook his hand, smiled, and told him: "The dame invites you for the wake, old chap."

Mike brightened instantly, clapped Will on the back and told him: "You did a great job there, Will. I'm proud of you, son."

"I'm Fred today. Don't forget," advised Will. "You can be whoever you want, quite frankly, except who you are. I hope you're good at improvisation and role-playing."

"Naughty, naughty," said Mike, pinching fondly Will's cheek.

A gravedigger had appeared from nowhere and stood leaning on his shovel by the tomb. He would wait until the mourners were out of sight before returning the earth to its rightful place. Then, it was off to the pub for him.

✳

Janet opened her front door to the sound of corks popping out of bottles.

She had not seen fit to tell the caterers of the nature of her reception. It was none of their business, after all, and she certainly didn't need any more people pretending to look tragic.

The approaching, smiling, black-clad waiters merged well with the guests, she thought, and brought an extra touch of elegance. And their timing had been excellent; they had clearly been on the lookout for her arrival. She was pleased about that.

Janet had distained to check whether she could get away with champagne at the event. Day by day she felt stronger in her resolve to eschew convention and decide things uniquely for herself. Only a brief, skeptical glance from her mother troubled her confidence as the bubbling wine tumbled into glasses in the entrance hall.

The guests came in, took drinks from the silver trays thrust before them, and fanned out into the salon, where a huge buffet lunch of only the finest dishes from the sea, the land and the skies awaited them.

"Get a scotch for the colonel, will you, please?" Janet instructed one of the waiters, pointing at Will. "And a large gin and tonic for me—no ice and heavy on the gin, if you would."

When all were safely inside the immense salon and everybody was holding a drink of one kind or another, Janet clapped her hands for silence.

"Welcome, my dear family and friends. I am very grateful to you all for coming today to see Ronald off with me."

She extracted a silk handkerchief from her jacket pocket and slowly dabbed her tear-filled eyes.

"Excuse me. I'm so sorry."

Could anyone except an English lady apologize for crying at her own husband's death? Strumpf wondered silently. "Vot a people!" he said under his breath.

Janet took a deep breath and continued: "Colonel Acton, his dearest friend, who I am especially pleased to see among us despite his recent trials, has spoken very eloquently of Ronald's immense qualities as a kind, generous, loving and cultured man. What can I possibly add to his fine words?

"All I would say right now is that I am sure … beyond any doubt at all … that if my husband were in any position to send us a message … he would ask you to smile and not weep … and would propose together with Shakespeare: *'Frame your mind to mirth and merriment, which bars a thousand harms and lengthens life'*. Yes, let us make merry, live long and suffer less!" she concluded with heartfelt conviction and warmth and a little choking laugh, raising her gin glass in toast.

At that, she invited them all to drink whatever and however much took their fancy and to throw themselves upon the lobster, the foie gras, the quail, the salmon, the stilton and the strawberries with gusto.

Is that it? thought Janet's mother.

It was indeed.

As others assaulted the buffet with enthusiasm, Mike discretely approached Mrs Chapman and whispered: "Satisfied client?"

The man lacked class, Janet decided. Couldn't he wait to carry out his customer approval survey, or whatever they called it?

She ignored his question. "How are you, Marlowe?"

"Can't complain. It's very nice of you to invite me to the party. I'm sorry for barging in on the funeral, but business is business, you know. I wanted to make sure my man made a good job of it."

"Quite."

Mike smiled. Well, I'm not going to get very far with the dame today, he thought, nodding his head slightly and moving off to an easier prey.

Will was looking with amazement at his sporting life.

"So, colonel, what's that?" asked Mike slyly, pointing at the middle of one of the photographs on the wall.

Will peered intently at the huge, dead beast he and Ronald were clutching and ventured: "A wild boar?"

"Very funny, 'Fred', very droll."

"No, no, I see now, the boat, the sea, the rods; couldn't be a wild boar, could it? I'd say it was a … fish."

"Bravo! It's a marlin, in fact," said Mike. "I caught one once, off the Canary Islands. Epic struggle. I don't know how the fish enjoyed the experience, but I was shagged, completely destroyed by the fight to land it. And then I was instructed to throw it back in the sea! Jesus! Don't you think, Fred, that fishing and throwing your catch back into the water is perhaps the most futile pursuit known to man? I was so appalled by this senseless act, I never fished again."

"So, you would rather have had the marlin stuffed and affixed to the wall of your living room?"

"That would have been quite something, I agree. But I would have been quite satisfied with having it smoked and eating it. Little by little, of course. It was so big it could have lasted a couple of years. What a waste."

They walked slowly past more pictures. Mike shook his head in wonderment. Will and Ronald drinking champagne on camp chairs as the sun went down over the Kenyan bush; Will and Ronald in tennis gear, each holding aloft in triumph a handle of their doubles trophy; Will and Ronald as students, face to face with books in their hands, smoking pipes and laughing gaily in a college study.

This is genius, thought Mike. Sheer genius. Perhaps I should bring Will in as an associate?

"Brilliant, Will, absolutely brilliant," whispered Mike. "I thought that I was thorough, a perfectionist, but this is taking our profession to another level altogether. How did you come up with the scheme?"

"Oh, it wasn't me. All the credit must go to Mrs Chapman. She got the idea from Stalin, apparently."

Both men looked across the salon as Janet moved among the guests, a smile here, a word there, a kiss on a cheek, a pat on a back.

Both men sighed and, though they didn't know it, had the exact same thought: "My God, what a beautiful woman."

Strumpf, meanwhile, was drinking as though he feared an impending drought. Feeling, quite rightly, that the professor was his entire responsibility, Will interrupted a conversation the old man was having with a waiter and pulled him to one side.

"Are you having a good time, Herr Professor?"

"Ja, ja, very gut! Ze only problem is zat people keep sinking I am a vaiter! Hahaha!"

At this, Strumpf took hold of his coat-tails and, with hilarity, flapped them out behind him. He then became suddenly serious:

"Vill, vy everyvon call you 'Fred'?"

"It's a long story, Herr Strumpf."

"Plees, Vill, call me Sigmund."

"I always wondered about your first name. It's Sigmund, then?"

"No, my name is Adolph—viz 'p-h', plees, but I like you call me Sigmund."

"Fine, today I'm Fred and you're Sigmund. Isn't it fun?"

Herr Strumpf understood nothing but didn't care in the slightest. He waved to a waiter he had befriended; the man arrived instantly with a cognac he had already poured in anticipation.

"Vielen Dank," said Strumpf to his new acquaintance.

"So, no slivovitz today, Sigmund? It would have been surprising to find it in an English mansion, it's true. But go easy, anyhow, if you want to keep on enjoying yourself."

"You're a very, very nice boy, Will-Fred," said Strumpf, throwing the brandy down his throat in one shot and slipping away to take some more lobster.

Having failed to interest the elusive Mrs Chapman in his presence, Mike had now attached himself to the only other beguiling women in the room, her three girlfriends.

He introduced himself to Sheila, Veronica and Sally as 'a friend of the colonel'. "The name's Marlowe, Mike Marlowe."

"Weren't your husbands with you?" he asked, seeing none of their men in the room any longer.

"Yes," laughed Veronica, "but after stuffing themselves with foie gras and stilton they slipped off; a 'very important' football match, apparently 'unmissable'."

"Yes, Arsenal-Tottenham," said Mike.

"So, what do you do in life?" asked Sally.

"I'm a detective."

"Good Lord!" said Veronica. "How interesting."

"A *private* detective," Mike added, restraining himself with difficulty from trying out his badly-mastered Bogart impersonation.

"Please, please, do tell us about your work," Sheila chipped in jauntily.

Mike spoke readily and inventively of his 'tails' on foot and his car chases at the wheel; of shadowy encounters in doorways with men and women investigating their philandering spouses; of hideouts; of reluctant witnesses who needed a little 'persuasion' to talk; of his video and audio spying devices; of the pitfalls and complexities of blackmail; of poking around at crime scenes after the cops had left; of his brushes with the law; and—the biggest, but far from only, lie—of his bullet and knife wounds.

The ladies were having a wonderful time, enlivening the discussion with the facile banter which comes so easily to middle-class English women and is certainly unequalled in the entire world.

Will, passing close by the little group on his way to get food and thus soak up some of the whisky he had been abusing, chuckled loudly to no one in particular: "*And the women come and go, talking of Michelangelo …*"

The ladies looked at him with resentment; they took the remark for themselves, though they didn't know what he meant. Mike too felt that Will was perhaps being unfriendly, though what his words might mean completely escaped him.

Each of the women thought silently the exact same thing: We'll fix his case a little later.

The Chapman family members, who had largely stuck together at the reception as they had at the grave-yard, gradually began to drift off. They had done their duty and it was time to leave the big city and get back to their comfortable and untroubled homes in the country. One by one or in pairs they bade farewell to Janet, wished her well and left.

Strumpf, finding himself unsteady on his feet, had installed himself in the middle of an epically long couch and was inviting any passing lady to join him. Janet was the first to take him up on his offer.

"So, a free consultation, Herr Doctor?"

"Nein, nein, nein!" protested a laughing Strumpf, lapsing into his native tongue as he did often when he was either happy or drunk, two things which, it was true, often coincided.

"Vonderful party, lovely funeral," the professor advanced. "I'm sorry."

"Thank you," said Janet politely. "Tell me, have you known Fred long?"

"Only today did I discover his name is Wilfred," mused Strumpf. "So, you never know everysing. But yes, ve see a very lot of each ozer. He's a very, very good boy."

"I was thinking that too," said Janet.

"Vot I can do is to interpret your dreams", he offered.

"I don't believe in that," said Janet. "And my dreams are so banal and uninteresting that you would really struggle. But I do have some excellent clients for you."

And with that Janet spoke loudly across the room: "Girls, come here, Sigmund is offering to analyze your dreams. Nothing too naughty, now."

Veronica, Sheila and Sally abandoned Mike without a word in the middle of one of his best stories, much to his chagrin, and threw themselves on the couch as Janet extricated herself.

With much gaiety and giggling, not least from Strumpf himself, a collective psychotherapy of night-time fantasies ensued. "I don't usually share my couch," Doctor Strumpf was heard to protest above the din. The ribald answers of the ladies were lost in raucous laughter. At one moment, Will came up behind Strumpf and whispered in his ear: "Perhaps you won't have to move to Nigeria after all, Sigmund."

Janet and Will found themselves alone in a corner.

A waiter had heard Mike talking about his life as a detective and as a keen reader of Dashiell Hammett had engaged him in conversation.

"He's stealing the show, your friend Sigmund," laughed Janet.

"He appears far from finished," said Will. He was right.

Suddenly, Strumpf roared gleefully across the room: "Is zere anybody here who ist who zey say zey are?"

Everybody laughed, though few understood. They took it as a professional reflection, an insight on the nature of being, or the Id, perhaps, from the distinguished psychoanalyst. Janet, as usual, thought of Sartre's waiter.

Strumpf then struggled to his feet, helped and held upright by the ladies, and proclaimed solemnly and sententiously: "*Aus so krummem Holze, als woraus der Mensch gemacht ist, kann nichts ganz Gerades gezimmert werden.*"

After a silence, Janet asked: "Anyone able and willing to translate?"

One of the waiters, the man who had become Strumpf's private purveyor of cognac, stepped forward, clearing his throat.

"May I?"

Sigmund stepped in and said: "Go ahead, Hans." And addressing himself to the remaining guests, added: "Hans is a poet and translator, you know. Go ahead, my friend."

Hans recited: "*Out of the crooked timber of humanity, no straight thing was ever made.*"

"My, that's so beautiful, so true ..." said Janet, bursting into uncontrollable tears.

"Kant," said Strumpf simply. "Dear old Kant."

CHAPTER FOURTEEN

Janet turned over in bed and walloped her sleeping companion in the nose with a fling of her outstretched arm.

"Ouch!" he protested.

She opened her eyes and came face to face with a man. "Will! What the hell are you doing here may I ask?"

"Well, you invited me actually," said Will apologetically. "I didn't have the strength to refuse, I'm afraid. I was so, so tired, not to mention three sheets to the wind."

They were both still dressed in their funeral attire.

"We didn't …?"

"No, Mrs Chapman, no we didn't. I had to put up quite a fight to save my honor, though."

"You liar! It's not possible!" she cried indignantly.

Will laughed gaily.

"I'm joking Mrs Chapman. Rectitude if not decorum was respected all round, as far as I can recall …"

"Thank God for that at least. But I must look absolutely awful. Turn your head immediately Will."

He rolled over happily. You are quite wrong, he thought; in its morning imperfections your beauty is even more breathtaking.

"Will you be a dear and go and prepare some coffee?" she said after a few minutes. "I'm going to make myself decent. I'll see you in the kitchen."

They each went their way. Will was already on his second cup by the time she reappeared. A stack of warm toast awaited her.

"I do think these are the most wonderful smells in the world, don't you, Will? Coffee and toast! They should bottle and sell them."

"I'm sure someone does already, Mrs Chapman."

"Will, please call me Janet. We have, after all, now 'spent the night together', as they say."

Will smiled.

"So, what did you think of the party? We pulled it off, didn't we? I must say your Strumpf was a great, unexpected success. A bit too fresh, perhaps, but otherwise I found him adorable. Detective Marlowe kept the girls amused, too, with his dark exploits in the pay of cuckolds. You, of course, were a triumph as the martial Colonel Acton and, though I say it myself, I thought I was the perfect grieving widow. I think I'll have to write a play about it all one day."

"And a pretty farce it would be," said Will.

"How did you find my girlfriends? They are such fun, aren't they? They all have so much bigger personalities than their husbands, that sorry trio of football-obsessed specimens."

"Yes, the girls were very lively," said Will. "They really kept me on my toes. I had to go way beyond the briefing that you gave me about Fred. In the end, I couldn't even remember whether I was repeating your falsehoods or making up new ones."

"What did they want to hear about?"

"I remember that one of them — Sheila, I think, she's the black-haired gypsyish-looking one, isn't she?"

"That's her. We even call her 'Carmen' when she gets a little wild ..."

"Well, Sheila wanted to know about my service in Afghanistan, specifically whether I had 'killed any Taliban'."

"Did you?"

"Well, I have now. I and some friends were coming back from a week-end of mountain climbing in the Hindu Kush when we were ambushed and had to fight our way out, leaving a dozen of the poor devils dead."

"Dear me."

"It was nice of you to have sent me on to Iraq, by the way; my feats of heroism there were even greater."

"You are not the youngest colonel in the British Army for nothing, Frederick Acton. But what else?"

"Inevitably, they wanted to know about your late husband. About my friendship with him. I spoke about the Oxford years, of course, about how our paths had diverged when he went into investment banking and I into the army. About how each time on leave from my distant missions, I sought him out and we renewed our friendship. About how we each in time got married. About how my own marriage had run into problems and the extraordinary support that he had given me through this very rough time."

"Did they ask you about him and me?"

"Not at all. They didn't seem curious at all about that. From loyalty, I would guess, wouldn't you? I suppose they thought that was none of my business."

"Perhaps," said Janet. "Though I have never considered discretion to be one of the virtues of my dear friends."

"Anyhow," continued Will, "I think that I sailed through all that. Though I was uneasy at moments, I have to confess."

"Why's that?"

"I don't know. The impostor syndrome?"

"Isn't that for people who actually have nothing to hide at all, who are honest and actually are what they present themselves to be?"

"Yes, you're right. But I demand that the real impostors should have the right to have their own syndrome too. When we start to believe that we are what we are not. I'm going to talk to my union about it."

They both laughed.

"No," Will continued, "what unnerved me a little was the feeling that your friends seemed to have some kind of private joke going on between them which I couldn't quite catch. Perhaps I'm paranoiac."

"I suppose that's a professional tic in your line," suggested Janet.

"In any case, we're not completely off the hook," she continued. "I hope you're free next Friday night. The girls demanded before they left that I should agree to maintain our weekly dinner—and they insisted that you should be there. They want it to be some kind of final tribute to Ronald. Sorry, but I accepted on your behalf. I'd really appreciate it, you know. Now that it's all over, they'll start to loosen up and seriously exercise their tongues, and I need the charming Colonel Acton to deflect a bit of their attention."

Against his better judgement, Will said 'yes'. He didn't know whether it was because he needed the employment or because saying 'no' to another evening with Mrs Chapman seemed beyond the realm of his abilities.

They chatted agreeably for a while longer, but soon both started to think about their duties in the day ahead.

Janet had to see the Coroner, to "tie up the last details," as his secretary had put it.

Will had to get home for a good bath and to change out of his ridiculously oversized black suit. He asked what he should do with it, whether he should have it cleaned before returning; Janet told him rather to get it burned, like Ronald's annals.

In truth, Will had not yet set fire to the notebooks, though he had told her that they had already gone to ashes. He wanted to read more of this unfortunate man's tale. You can't simply do away with a life with a box of matches, he thought.

"Honesty obliges me to remind you that you are still paying for me, you know," said Will on the threshold of the Chapman home.

"I know very well, Will. But let's let it run a bit. I

need the support and perhaps you wouldn't mind the work."

To his surprise, she kissed his cheek in farewell.

CHAPTER FIFTEEN

He had eaten a very fine lunch. The little Corbières he had selected to accompany the venison had been just perfect. In the good old style, he thought, fast being abandoned under market forces, the tastes of the fainthearted, or some such rubbish; smokey, intensely spicy, outrageously tannic. It had quite put the meat in the shade.

Bathing in the glow of his postprandial wellbeing, Wordsworth the Coroner didn't feel at all inclined to beat about the bush. He thus asked abruptly:

"Can you tell me about your sex life?"

"Most certainly not!" said Janet indignantly. "What kind of a question is that?"

"With your late husband, I mean."

"With whom *else*? What on earth are you implying?"

She will quite destroy my mood, thought Wordsworth.

"It's necessary for my enquiry."

"I cannot for the life of me understand why."

"I assure you that I need to know before signing off on the case."

What an infamy, thought Janet, examining this fat-bellied, grinning Falstaff up and down with her most withering look.

"Well, if you *really* require such information, I

would say that we had the normal life of a happily married couple," she lied.

"Your husband died of a heart attack," he resumed, looking at a paper on his desk.

"Yes, so I was told by the hospital."

"Was there a history of heart disease in his family?"

"As a matter of fact, yes. Both his parents and even his young brother were struck down prematurely by attacks. But he hadn't shown any sign of coronary problems, as far as I know."

"Quite, quite," said the coroner.

"Did he jog?"

"Good Lord, no."

"Any other sport?"

Janet shook her head. "Not in recent times."

"Which brings me back to my original enquiry about your ... your ... your ..."

"Fornication?" suggested Janet with disdain.

"I do have to ask," repeated Wordsworth.

"You're not implying that we were ... that we were ... *on the job* at the time, as it were, are you?" She wished she had been able to find another expression, but none had come to her rescue.

"No, no," laughed the Coroner inappropriately.

"Nothing of the sort. But the autopsy found large traces of Sildenafil citrate in his blood."

"From his sleeping pills, I suppose?"

"No, that's the problem. Sildenafil is the active ingredient of erectile dysfunction drugs."

"Erectile *what*?!" grimaced Janet.

"Dysfunction. Not rising to the occasion, as it were."

Janet sat in puzzled silence. What was this awful man getting at?

"To put it in a nutshell, Mrs Chapman, your husband died from a heart attack provoked by an overdose of Viagra or some similar product."

"Good God."

"You didn't *know* that he was taking such pills, then? He was doing it in secret? You hadn't noticed any 'dysfunction', shall we say?"

Janet, stunned, shook her head slowly from side to side, both as a response to Coroner Wordsworth and in perplexity about what she was hearing.

"I thought about holding an inquest," he continued. "But I've decided against it. The medical report is cut and dried; there's no doubt as to the causes of death. It wouldn't be useful at all. I must say, however, it's the very first case of its kind in my humble career. I've come across plenty of overdose deaths, deliberate and perhaps otherwise, but never with the use of Viagra, I must say. Sleeping pills, certainly, paracetamol, often, anti-depressants, from time to time ..."

Janet had ceased to listen. In a stupor, confused and bewildered, she had to bring an immediate end to this sordid story. She interrupted the coroner's fond overdose reminiscences, signed blindly a document he put into her hand, stood up and walked silently out of his office without so much as a goodbye.

Wordsworth looked after her with a little resentment at this lack of respect for his high office, but above all with his first thoughts about the dinner with which he would regale himself that evening. Perhaps a turbot? He had spotted an exciting little Cévennes white on the wine card that he was really keen to taste.

CHAPTER SIXTEEN

"Will, can I ask you a really awful, *frightful* question?"

"Shoot," said Will.

"Will, don't speak like that; you're clearly spending far too much time with Marlowe. That language doesn't suit you at all."

"Sorry. I meant to say 'Je vous en prie, Madame'."

"That's much better.

"I'm really not sure how I can ask you this, but I have no men close to me, not a single one, actually. And this is not a subject I could discuss with the girls; they wouldn't know a thing about it, apart from anything else.

"Please forgive me, but this is what I need to know: When a man doesn't have a love life, in an onanistic moment, if I could put it that way, could you ever imagine him taking Viagra? For himself, I mean?"

"That is quite possibly the most unusual and perhaps most challenging question I have ever been asked," laughed Will.

Janet did not look amused in the slightest, so he went on soberly: "I really have no idea, no idea at all. I don't think it's impossible, logically, but I really have no clue. If it's important for you to know, I could ask around at the bar."

I certainly know a prize wanker or two among the clients, he joked to himself. But why on earth was she asking him the question?

"No, don't do that, Will, it's not becoming at all. You'll get in trouble with the management. I'm amazed that I even had the bad taste to ask you, but it's become very important for me to know. Maybe I'll look it up on the Internet."

"I don't at all wish to be nosy or prying, Janet, but it's a really bizarre question, particularly coming from you. Perhaps if you told me what inspires you to ask, I could try and help?"

Janet hesitated. And then acquiesced. "Yes, why the hell not, Will. You have, after all, practically become my confidant. You're the only single person to know the whole truth about any of this wretched business. Isn't that amazing? You are the only friend I can trust. And I'm paying you!"

"*There's no trust, no faith, no honesty in men. All perjured, all forsworn, all naught, all dissemblers,*" she inveighed. "What a world. Did I really find an honest man? That's how Mike described you, you know. Believe it or not he's actually read Hamlet, 'as part of my research', he said."

Yes, I'm honest, thought Will. It never did me any good that I can remember, but I am this way and must live with it, even though some consider that I am a fool, I know very well. How fantastic though that she considers me to be a 'friend'! I would gladly tear up my contract with Extra! and start all over again for that.

"So here's the story, Will my boy. I went to the coroner yesterday, as you know. Awful, awful man, you cannot imagine. A real pig. In any case, he confirmed that Ronald's heart attack was undoubtedly provoked by an overdose. One can never be sure, of course, but everything points to that."

"Sleeping pills?" asked Will politely.

"Precisely *not*," said Janet. "That's been the assumption, my assumption at least, all along. Indeed, I actually found a box of them, quite empty, lying next to his body, so it seemed completely obvious. But that is not at all what they found in his blood. They rather found strong traces of some chemical or other whose name I have already forgotten but which turns out to be the main component of *Viagra* or somesuch product.

"Well, Will, I have to confess to you that Ronald and I hadn't been 'sleeping together', to use the euphemism, for a very long time …"

"I now understand your question."

"Indeed."

He was even more anxious now to find some time to go on reading the diaries.

CHAPTER SEVENTEEN

"I had Strumpf followed," Mike told Will.

"You did *what*?"

"Yes, I was curious. Got an old colleague to do the job. He owed me one. He tailed him out of your bar, where he'd been on the lookout for a couple of days.

"He says you make a wicked margarita, by the way. But you're bloody expensive. I had to pick up his expense tab and it knocked me back a fair few dozen quid, I can tell you."

Will remembered the flatfoot well.

"I know the man. He said he was an insurance salesman."

"Yeah, good cover that, we use it often. No one knows what insurance salesmen look like, after all. And no one likes them either, so they don't have many people engaging in conversation and sticking their noses into their real business."

"Anyhow, Mike, why on earth would you follow Strumpf? What's he to you?"

"I guess you could say it was professional interest. Look, I know that all psychoanalysts are phonies, but I thought to myself as we chatted at the wake: 'This guy is a fake phoney, not a real phoney'. I just had to find out whether my instincts were right or not. While we're curious, we're still alive, I always say."

"But what did he say that made you doubt? He looks

and speaks like what he says he is, doesn't he?"

"Well, that's probably what made me suspicious. My detective friend looks like an insurance salesman, as you quite correctly pointed out. You look as much like a colonel in the British Army as my aunt Sally.

"But I'm not a colonel in the British Army," Will protested.

"Proves my point!" said Mike cockily.

It proves nothing at all, thought Will, except that you're getting lost in your own psychological dialectics.

Mike resumed: "Look, here we have this shabby-looking Viennese womanizer—he even made me appear like a picture of restraint—who can barely speak English, who can't make up his mind whether he's called Sigmund or Adolf ..."

"Adolph with p-h, by the way," Will intervened. "But how do you know that?"

"I heard him introducing himself to the German waiter as 'Adolf'; we're trained to keep our eyes and ears open, you know."

"Perhaps. But we were practically all using bogus names that day," Will exaggerated. I was 'Fred', you were 'Marlowe' ..."

"Proves my point, Will my boy," he insisted. "One more false identity wouldn't at all have been out of place!"

"You've been seeing too many old movies, Mike."

"That's as may be, Will. But as you may remember, old 'Strumpf'—if that's his name—was pretty plastered, to put it mildly, and started saying very bizarre things to me. Rather than clarifying whether he was 'Adolf' or 'Sigmund', he actually asked me to call him 'Svengali'! At one moment he thrust forward his ugly mug so that our noses were practically touching—I almost fell over from the fumes—and whispered to me: 'You vill now do vot I say'. It was very creepy, Will."

"So you had him followed? Mike, you amaze me."

Mike took this as a compliment and smiled broadly.

"And what did you discover, if anything?"

"That, I am not going to tell you, Will old boy. I want you to find out for yourself. Here's an address, go look," said Mike, handing him a piece of paper.

The address was in the West End, just off the Strand. Will knew the area well and thought he had even heard of the street name.

"How is Mrs Chapman?" asked Mike as Will left the agency. "She's still paying us, you know; you're still working. It's the longest job we've ever done. I guess we're into after sales service too."

Will could really have done without Mike's heavy wink, but he too wondered why he was still being employed. He had even been summoned again by Mrs Chapman that very evening.

In the meantime, he headed for the West End in some trepidation. Did Dr Strumpf live, after all, in an asylum, as he had long suspected? Was he really mad?

Will got out of the Underground at Leicester Square, consulted the street map of the area, and found the address a short walk away towards the Strand.

He was soon there. The building housed not an asylum but a small theater; it was shut and plunged in darkness. But billboards on both sides of the entrance told their story:

Star of the Salzburg Palladium
The Sensational Sigmund Strumpf's Theater of Magic
Come in and be Hypnotized!

Performances took place from Wednesday to Saturday at eight and ten o'clock.

CHAPTER EIGHTEEN

So, Strumpf was not a psychoanalyst but a hypnotist. Good Lord, thought Will, he's an actor and an impostor too. No wonder we get on so well. I shall never tell him I know, though. I couldn't bear for him to be hurt; he's already fragile and unhappy. If he dissimulates his real life, it must be for a reason. And one must respect a man's secrets. Perhaps, in time, he will talk about it, but it's for him to choose the moment. If only Mike could remain discrete; though there is nothing less likely than that.

Will was at home, contemplating a stack of notebooks on his table. Here, too, he wondered whether he was right to be poking around in a man's life when the man had done him no harm, when he didn't even know him, actually. He couldn't decide whether the fact that the man was dead made it better or worse.

I must do it for Janet, he thought. The bankers at the funeral had behaved very decently and had not said a word to her about Ronald's premature disappearance from their midst. But it was bound to come out, as she tied up all his affairs in the weeks and months to come. Perhaps, if I have an explanation, I can attenuate her suffering about this duplicity which she has never suspected.

Will flicked through the pages of the diaries looking for references to work and the bank among the philosophical observations, bon mots and reflections about the struggle to live and love. He finally found one:

A Monday stolen from the office, devising strategies for survival.

And a few pages on:

I told Janet about my disgust with the firm and with my job. She says the exact words I do not want to hear: "It's done us very well indeed, Ronald, don't knock it dear. Everyone gets tired of his work from time to time, even the Pope—or the Queen—I'm sure. You'll feel better about it again soon. Do make an effort."

Ronald clearly despaired of her cheerful admonitions.

I cannot abide optimists—and I'm married to one! What greater cruelty is there than to tell an unhappy man that he is mistaken in his suffering? That his cure lies merely in a change of attitude! I loathe the bank; never want to see another investment proposal, prospectus, balance sheet, merger and acquisition analysis; never want again to sell equity, stocks, organize IPOs. May this whole wretched world collapse and leave me in peace.

And a few lines later:

Perhaps I could actually orchestrate the bank's downfall? That should be possible. Perhaps I could bring down the whole system, in fact? Cause chaos in stock markets, a run on the pound and the dollar, panic among lenders … In banking as in practically every sphere of human activity, a single man can make mighty institutions fall and cause havoc across the whole planet.

Ronald's dreams of causing the next economic apocalypse had gone on for a few more paragraphs like this and then ceased. Personally, Will was grateful that the man apparently hadn't had the required energy to bring down the world financial system. He had rather turned to his own life again:

Intellectually, I am a grotesque failure … nothing but a tiny echo of thinking already thought, of ideas already ideated, of philosophy already philosophized. I have nothing to add at all to the words with which great men have wrought truths from our condition.

"How weary, stale, flat and unprofitable seem to me all the uses of this world." Yes, indeed, Hamlet having said it five hundred years ago, What's left to add? What's left to say? What's left to do?

Christ, this is depressing, thought Will. He nevertheless read on. At the turn of a page, he found what he had been seeking:

Finita la commedia! I shall not spend one more day, one more hour, dying a slow, dull death at the bank. I am not J. Alfred Prufrock! It's over. I shall never return, never!

Will could not find a single other reference to the bank from that point on. So, it was apparently as Ronald's former colleague had told him. He simply disappeared from the office without telling anyone anything. And five months later he had killed himself.

There were still three volumes that he had not even opened. What might they contain? wondered Will. A slow descent into despair and misery and the final decision, he supposed. He read the first page of the next notebook; he had found what he needed to know and would put the whole sad story aside after that.

The notebook began with a summing up:

I have abandoned my professional career; my marriage is practically over; I am not a thinker or a poet and my illusions of a new intellectual life lie in ashes.

These gloom-laden considerations were followed by an indictment of Homo sapiens that Will thought not badly expressed at all:

The tragedy of modern man is not that he knows less and less about the meaning of his life, but that it bothers him less and less. So what to do? I know. I shall call V …

*

It was three o'clock in the morning. Will sat staring at the wall, his hand resting on the last page of the last notebook of the annals of Ronald Chapman.

He was stunned. Of all the things he might have found, he did not expect for an instant to chance upon the three-volume memoirs of the Casanova of Kensington. The man had indeed resolved the dilemma of filling a life emptied of work, marriage and thought.

Will had not read anything so licentious and immoral in his entire life.

CHAPTER NINETEEN

"Do you think it's justified to lie if you do so to protect people?"

"Most certainly!" said Janet with conviction.

"*We have art so as not to perish from the truth*," she declaimed.

"Shakespeare?" asked Will.

"No, Nietzsche, I believe. Lying in order to flatter or to be kind to someone is perfectly warranted too, in my opinion. Particularly if it's to me; I love it!"

"And if one later tells the truth, does it cancel out the lie? Or does telling the truth then make the lie culpable?"

"I give up. Get to the point, Will—to whom have you been lying, you naughty fellow? Apart from everyone, that is."

"I lied to you, Janet, but I'm afraid that to tell you the truth now might be much worse than that original sin."

"Come, come. Out with it. You have to now, anyhow, you honest man. I can't possibly think that you have been venal. I can take it, particularly since it apparently troubles your conscience."

"I didn't burn Ronald's diaries as I told you I had."

She laughed.

"I understand, Will. Forget it. I really don't care, you know. Don't chastise yourself about that for a second.

Get rid of them how and when you like. If you're masochistic enough to want to read more of them, go ahead. Just don't bring the subject up with me again, that's a good boy. As I told you, I don't want to hear a word about their contents. Nothing beneficial could possibly come of it; just knives turning endlessly in old wounds. Would you like a scotch?"

"Indeed I would! A double," he said with enthusiasm.

As she left the room, Will wondered if he should give up there. To hurt this woman with Ronald's story would be a very great sacrilege. If she knew it, on the other hand, it might kill all the regret that she might ever have about him, their marriage and his death. She has been so bold, so courageous, so discrete about these things, he thought. Perhaps she is suffering much more than I or any of us can guess? What a dilemma.

"Well, here's to a new life!" toasted Janet as she came into the salon bearing their usual drinks.

Will had decided, for better or for worse, to tell her the truth.

"There's a little unfinished business to settle first, I think, before you start your new life."

"What might that be?"

"I think that I can explain the Viagra."

"Really?" said a surprised Janet. "You've been asking around then, after all?"

"No, the explanation is in the last volumes of Ronald's notebooks. Or so I think."

Janet sat silently, looking at Will intently. She didn't need to ask him to go on.

Will gulped down the rest of his whisky, poured himself a new one from the bottle Janet had left on the table in front of him, and said: "He was having an affair with Sheila."

Janet did not react and just stared at him.

"And with Sally."

Still, Janet did not as much as flinch.

"And with Veronica."

Janet rose silently, left the salon and climbed the stairs without a word. Will could hear her sobbing in the bedroom above him.

❋

The light dimmed as afternoon turned to evening. For a long while now, the only sound in the house came from a huge, dark, ugly grandfather clock in the corner of the salon. What-have-you-done? What-have-you-done? What-have-you-done? Will asked over and over again, unable to free himself from the clock's infernal, accusatory tick-tock-tick-tock mantra. He looked at the empty bottle on the table, as though it might give him the answer, and wondered whether there was any more whisky in the house.

Staring into virtual darkness now, he realized for the first time that he was in love. That he had been in love, in fact, since the moment she had opened the front door to him in this very house and called him, in that low, husky voice that he adored, 'Fred'. I love the way she walks, I love the way she talks, he recited to himself mindlessly, echoing the refrain from a hundred long-forgotten pop songs. I love her fiery red hair, the way she throws it to the winds with that fierce backward jerk of her head; I love her reckless, raucous laughter; I love her candor, her directness, her lapses of diplomacy; I love her shyness with sentiments, her modesty with feelings; I love her gaiety, her joy for life, her bravery with death, her courage to face down the world, her resolve to do what she wants to do and to be happy come what may ...

"I even love her *teeth*!" he said out loud to his own laughter. "It's true!"

He heard noises from upstairs. Doors opening and closing, water running, a voice.

After a while, a light came on in the staircase and then another just outside the salon.

"Colonel Acton, you are taking me dancing," Janet said gruffly from the hallway. "That's an order!"

And in she walked. A sight to behold, a vision of beauty, thought Will. Her hair tied up in a bun transversed by a jeweled stick; a pearl necklace gracing her lovely neck and pearls too hanging from her perfect ears; a low-cut dark orange dress brought in at her slender waist with a red belt; tiny glittering silver stars sprinkled on her face and bare arms. A radiant smile.

"Don't just stare, Will. Say 'Janet Chapman, you look absolutely gorgeous!'"

With this, she spun round upon herself and stood still in front of him, arms akimbo.

"Janet Chapman, you look absolutely gorgeous," he said earnestly.

"That's better. I'm really going to have to train you how to talk to a woman, my boy. To think you're supposed to be a professional boyfriend! Those girls are definitely being short-changed. Good God, you've a lot to learn.

"Now, go and get freshened up, on the double. Take your pick of the old bugger's clothes — at least a clean shirt—that's a good chap. I've laid out a selection on the bed in my room.

"I've booked for dinner at the Savoy first. I don't know about you, but I'm absolutely famished. Then I know a nice little jazz club in Camden. Sound like a good programme?"

Will smiled, nodded happily and went silently, obediently, upstairs. What a woman, he was thinking, what a woman.

＊

As, bent in two, he ducked and followed her into the back seat of the chauffeured car she had hired for the evening, she leant over and kissed him lightly on his forehead.

"Thank you, Will."

First my cheek, now my brow; moving closer, thought Will, as Janet took out her handkerchief and removed her lipstick trace.

"The Savoy, Charles, please, we're starving hungry!" Janet commanded.

"I'm Fred," replied the chauffeur amiably.

"Two Freds for the price of one!" cried Janet cheerfully. "No offense, but you should really be called Charles, you know, in your line of work."

The driver laughed as the car moved off. "You may call me Charles, Madame, no problem at all. Be my guest. So your name is Fred too, Sir?"

"Only on Sundays and Fridays," said Will.

The chauffeur chuckled heartily; he didn't know why, except that they were encouraged to find the clients amusing. It was part of the job.

✻

The dinner had been a bit of a trial for Will. Though he drew on his best role-playing and improvisational skills, of course, he was unused to dining in such casual opulence, with waiters bowing and scraping around him, and was uncomfortable, not least physically, wearing a dead man's oversized clothes. He did like, however, that the maître d'hôtel, a Frenchman, addressed him as often as possible as 'Mon Colonel'.

Janet, on the other hand, was in her element, trying the patience of the waiters to its furthest limit with changes to her orders and disobliging remarks about the temperature of the wine and the cooking of the meat.

Will watched her performance and that of the complicit waiters with admiration for everyone and a renewed and deep love of life, his life, that is.

They were both happy now to relax in the small and lively club where 'Charles' had taken them from the Savoy on Janet's instructions. The rum cocktails were excellent, they had a little table by the dance floor, the band was good but left space to talk, even though they were both silent.

Janet had managed through sheer will to put a certain case of the most terrible treachery out of her mind for several hours. She had not said a word about it to Will all evening.

Now I am ready, she thought, taking Will's hand and pulling him off to dance once more.

Having earlier improvised and imitated—not too badly, he thought—what Janet told him was a creole dance called zydeco, having jived and jitterbugged, and performed various swing shags, the exhausted Will was enormously relieved to hear the band begin a mournful blues, the sign for a good old hip-to-hip, chest-to-chest smooch.

Janet laid her head on Will's shoulder and plotted vengeance. Those witches shall regret to their dying day that they betrayed me, she swore to herself, whispering in Will's loving ear: "*I'll never pause again, never stand still, till either death hath closed these eyes of mine or fortune given me measure of revenge.*"

After a moment, she added: "Though in fact, Will, fortune will not have to wait any longer than Friday night."

She broke off their dance and led him back to the table. "But are you still up for it, Will, Friday night? It will take strong nerves, you know. It won't be particularly pleasant. It will also be your last performance as Colonel Acton. It's all over after that. Will you come?"

Will feigned, hypocritically, to hesitate, particularly since he had decided earlier in the day that he would follow her to the very ends of the earth if she had any use for him, and said simply: "Yes."

"You realize also that they must be aware you're not Fred, not Acton, not a colonel, not an alpine climber, not a near-suicide?"

"I hadn't thought. You're right, of course."

"And that they knew it already when you were recounting your battle glories at the wake? That they were laughing in your face, in my face too, while harboring their dirty little secrets. That they let me tell all those stories about you at our weekly parties, while mocking me behind my back. I wonder if they knew about each other, though? They're going to find out now, that I promise."

Yes, I was Ronald's alibi, thought Will. Another Extra! rule I've broken. Mike had been very clear about that. But I don't think he had dead men in mind, so I'm sure it's OK now.

"I'm with you all the way, Janet," resumed Will, laying his hand gently upon hers on the table and burning his palm on her illicitly lit cigarette. "Ouch!" They laughed and she called for the bill.

❀

Chapter Nineteen

As they drove up to Janet's home, Will asked her discretely if the car was still good to take him home. She ignored his question and pushed him out on the pavement and into the house.

She took him by the hand and led him directly up the stairs.

CHAPTER TWENTY

"*The play's the thing wherein I'll catch the conscience of the king.* Or rather the conscience of three strumpets. I intend to roast them very slowly, Colonel Acton. I hope you've learnt well your lines?"

"Yes, of course. I'm sure they'll come *trippingly on the tongue.*"

She laughed. "Good boy! *Be not too tame neither, but let your discretion be your tutor. Suit the action to the word, the word to the action, with this special observance that you o'erstep not the modesty of nature.*"

"I'll do me best to act natural-like, ma'am," he assured her in his best country bumpkin accent.

'Charles' was chuckling at the wheel. "Are you actors then, if you don't mind me asking?"

"Tonight, yes, every one of us," was all Janet would offer as a reply.

As they drove through the dusk towards Veronica's Hampstead home, which for geographical convenience had become the permanent venue for their weekly dinners, Janet cast her mind back over the friendship the four women had enjoyed for so many years.

She had met them individually, in different circumstances, and it had been her initiative to bring them, one by one, together. What had they shared? Apart from her husband, that is! A determination, perhaps, to be happy? They were all sharp, witty, lively, joyful, in-

telligent ... what else could you ask of friends? She
wanted nothing of bitter, acrimonious, troubled or
mournful women complaining of their frustrations or
their husbands or anything else, come to that, and they
had all tacitly agreed to be nothing but positive with
each other. Their friendship was uniquely a place for
sunshine and happiness and laughter; each of them
could just go elsewhere if she needed psychotherapy.
Of course, thought Janet, they must have had their
problems, as indeed she had too, but that was not the
point of their comradeship, their camaraderie. And it
had all been enormous fun and pleasure.

But the bitches had been shagging Ronald! Not even
in the open, as it were, but behind her back. For that,
she would never pardon them. She didn't give a damn
what anyone else thought about forgiveness. For her,
it was a completely useless, unworthy emotion that led
to nothing at all and demanded only that victims should
pay a higher price than their violators. They had betrayed her, made a fool of her; they had condemned
themselves to her eternal indifference and to their obliv-
ion. They could live their sad lives without her, that was
for sure. She was made of different stuff; she was loyal;
she had in her way stuck to Ronald right to the bitter
end; she had done her best; she had never betrayed him,
nor was it ever even within the bounds of possibility
that she might have done so.

"What are you thinking, Will dear?" she asked in
order to break out of the tormented circle of her own
thoughts.

"About acting," he lied; "about how it's so much easier in life than on the stage."

He had indeed again been thinking about this enigma, but earlier, before she had picked him up from his home. He wasn't nervous at all and did not fear in the slightest his forthcoming evening as Colonel Acton, not even now he understood that Janet's friends knew him to be a phoney. For some mysterious reason that he could not quite grasp, the whole situation had become even more remarkably interesting. The girls all knew from Ronald that he was a fake, certainly. But they did not know that he knew that they knew; they presumably did not even know that one another knew about him, since they knew nothing about each other's affairs. In a sense, he was now doubly if not triply free … he could be and say what he wished, improvise at will, as before, but with no latent threat at all that he might be caught out, exposed, because the women could not admit their knowledge of the deception to anyone without unmasking themselves to Janet, to him, to each other and, not least, to their husbands. Pirandello could have written it, he thought.

Now, though, in the car, Will thought only of the woman sitting next to him, 'the extraordinary Mrs Janet Chapman', as he called her to himself and as she would doubtless forever be known within his heart. Ten days ago, he had not been aware of her existence. Today, they were on the cusp of an unfathomable and unthinkable romantic adventure. There had been no great declarations of sentiment or devotion, let alone of love. She had simply said "Come away with me, Will, come away with me to foreign lands." He had said, simply, 'Yes', and they had sealed their fate with a kiss.

Janet also was thinking about what had happened to them, was thinking about this man, this stranger, with whom she planned to spend the next chapter of her life. He was a rock, she had decided, and what she needed in her life right now was exactly that, a solid, unmovable rock. He was not dull, not for an instant; but he was not open to all the winds of fancy that could sweep through a man's mind; he was not the kind, she thought, to question the foundations even of his existence. He was, when all was said and done, and this was not for a moment a criticism, satisfied with his lot and resolutely optimistic. He took life as it came to him, or so it seemed to her, and she thought that this was wonderful, remarkable and perhaps even unusual. She would be the dreamer. One was more than enough in a couple.

"*Give me that man that is not passion's slave, and I will wear him in my heart's core, ay, in my heart of heart, as I do thee,*" she recited to herself.

"Good, dear Will," she said out loud, à propos of nothing at all.

He turned and smiled at her warmly, but felt obliged to say: "Are you sure that you want to go through with this, Janet? We could just as well drive off elsewhere, you know, go and eat alone, go and dance if you'd like to."

"No, Will. *You must be proud, bold, pleasant, resolute.*

And now and then stab, when occasion serves. Tonight, I must stab!"

"Shakespeare?" asked Will.

"No, Marlowe."

"Mike?"

"No, no, no," she laughed gaily. "Christopher, the man some claim faked his own murder to escape persecution for blasphemy and reappeared under the assumed name 'Shakespeare'. You only have to read Marlowe's plays to know that this is rubbish," she said confidently. "Quite inferior."

As Hampstead neared, Will had doubts, questions, qualms about one thing only: the men who were shortly to discover that they had been sold down the river, castrated, swindled out of their tranquil lives, and now would face months and years, even whole lives, perhaps, of humiliation and regret. He took no pleasure whatsoever in their downfall, no more than in that of their adulterous wives. As a man, he did not feel any particular solidarity with them either. He had always thought, based on no personal experience or evidence at all, that if a man were to make a woman happy, she would be loyal to him. This was perhaps complete rubbish, he conceded. He was certainly not ready to give men credit for similar faithfulness, particularly from his observations working in bars for the last fifteen years ...

"We're here," the driver announced. "What time would you like me to pick you up? You can call me whenever you like, of course."

"Don't wander too far, Charles," Janet instructed. "This might be a very short evening. No one yet knows."

✻

The three husbands were shiftily eyeing a football match on a television in the corner of the room while half-heartedly and distractedly engaging in conversation with Will.

"Please go ahead and watch—don't mind me," he said to put them at ease. "What's the game?"

It was Porto against Benfica, they told him. An exciting, vital match that would decide the outcome of the Portuguese championship.

Will laughed. "Oh, it's *that* important. Please do watch," he urged again. "As long as you keep my scotch topped up, you can ignore me completely." They needed no more encouragement than that. One handed him the whisky bottle and all three turned full square to the screen.

It was silent in the rest of the house. Perhaps Janet has poisoned them? he wondered. He then heard wild shrieks—no, she's cutting them to pieces with kitchen knives, clearly.

"Now put that off," ordered Veronica, marching into the room with a tray of steaming food, followed by Sally, Sheila and Janet carrying many other dishes. The obedient men sighed volubly as one of them got up and cut the picture and sound, all the while double-checking that the recording function remained set.

The girls spread the bowls, plates and platters across the table. The guilty men, having left all preparations until then to their women, made faint-hearted efforts to help this last-minute organization but were pushed aside without ceremony.

"I hope that you're not as useless at home as our men are," Sally told Will.

Will laughed. "Well, I cook a lot, actually, and even clear up afterwards. Or rather did, before I and my wife separated. I hope she gets comparable service from her lover," he added solemnly.

The others looked awkwardly at each other but said nothing as they took their places at the table.

"Janet, Fred, what would you like?" asked Veronica with a sweep of her arm across the feast of dishes.

"The toad looks good," observed Janet. "Yes, please pass me the toad if you would."

"That's wool of bat and tongue of dog isn't it?" Will asked, pointing at a dark dish of stew. "Or perhaps I'll take fingers of birth-strangled babes?" he conjectured, indicating a plate of shrimps. "Yes, I think I'll start with them."

"The Turk's nose with Tartar's lips is very fresh too, Fred," Janet added helpfully.

"*Toad*?" asked Sheila's husband, emerging suddenly from his football stupor. "You made *toad*?"

"Now don't be stupid, Peter, our friends are having a little literary joke."

"These men have four things in common, as far as I can see," Will remembered Janet telling him. "Not the slightest trace of culture of any kind; a tremendous talent for making lots of money—they all run their own businesses; an insane passion for football; and a complete lack of wits." To which could now be added their shared cuckoldery, thought Will as he looked at them gobbling down their food.

"How are you bearing up, Janet?" asked Sheila kindly. "The wake was fantastic, by the way."

"I'm fine, thanks. I miss him very much, of course," she lied.

"Yes, of course, we all do", said Sally.

I bet you do, you worthless, cheating whores, thought Janet.

"Fred has been of great support to me, though."

Will could swear that he saw Sheila wink discretely at Sally. What on earth could *that* mean? Only, perhaps, that in their philandering minds they supposed that the fake Colonel Acton was in fact Janet's lover? We do suspect in others the replication of our own sins, he philosophized.

"We're very happy indeed that you could join us tonight, colonel," said Veronica. "We're only sorry that the circumstances are so tragic. Janet told us an awful lot about your friendship with Ronald. We can only reproach you a little for taking him away from us so often at our weekly parties these past months."

Bloody good thing, each of the husbands thought separately. Fucking intellectual! one cursed. Believed he was superior! reflected another. Didn't even know Arsène Wenger! said the still-astonished third man to himself.

How do people lie so easily and so brazenly? wondered Janet. It must really be in our genes, she thought. Everyone is lying to everyone. What a species! We must have got it from the monkeys, she speculated. Now *that* was a good subject for table talk …

"I saw a fascinating documentary film the other day about how monkeys lie to each other," said Janet suddenly.

"Tell us about it," Will encouraged her.

"There was this troop of monkeys who scavenge their food on the banks of a river. When one of them sees a poisonous snake slide out of the water, it screams "Snake, snake!"—in monkey language, of course—and they all scarper up the nearest tree. However, these treacherous animals are also observed to shout exactly the same thing when they chance on a piece of food, a dead fish for example. They cry "Snake, snake!" then too. All their mates flee up the trees and hide trembling in the branches, leaving the lying monkey to eat his fish in peace without having to fight them over it."

"Fascinating," said Will. "Much like humans in many ways."

"I don't see the parallel, personally," said Peter.

"Never mind, dear," said his wife, before going on to speculate about consciousness in other forms of life. Trees were said to think, she seemed to recall. Even to communicate with each other. Did *they* also lie? she asked.

"To be is to lie," said Janet somberly. "It's inescapable. I personally don't even have a problem with it; quite the contrary. What's unpardonable is not lying, but betraying, cheating on someone, a spouse, for instance, or a friend."

Like Horatio at Hamlet's play within a play, Will kept a keen look on the reaction of the women to Janet's words. They showed nothing, nothing that he could perceive at least.

After the women had all exhausted their knowledge, which admittedly was slim, about the consciousness of animals, trees, plants—even stones, ventured one of them—and one of the men had provoked a good laugh with his buddies about the lack of any discernible consciousness or even brain activity in the Tottenham goalkeeper when Ramsey's rocket shot had flown past his immobile figure into the net and won the match for Arsenal the previous week, they turned back to the recently deceased, whom they were supposed to be celebrating.

"I propose a toast to Ronald, to his memory," said Veronica.

"Ronald," echoed around the table.

"We all rather lost sight of him these last several months," lied Sally, "but he was never forgotten and never shall be."

I've had quite enough of this lying bullshit, thought Janet, deciding it was time to move in for the kill.

At that moment, however, Veronica got up and said she had to go and get further dishes.

"*Away, and mock the time with fairest show,*" Janet called after her. "*False face must hide what the false heart doth know.*"

"Whatever that might mean," muttered Veronica.

Will suspected, and Janet shared his thought, that they perhaps had finally touched a nerve.

When Veronica was again seated and began doling out Sheila's famous sherry trifle in bowls, Janet struck.

"Ronald kept a diary, you know. He wrote down absolutely everything about his life."

The men paid no attention to this useless information and went on chatting between themselves, but an uncanny silence fell over the three women.

"Oh really," said Sally. "Anything interesting in them?"

"I haven't read them yet. It's been such a very busy two weeks," Janet replied.

The respite and relief were practically tangible.

"But Fred has, though. And he tells me that it recounts a little tale in which you are all characters. Isn't that fascinating?"

The women said nothing and stared deeply into their trifle. None of them touched it.

Janet launched into a soliloquy:

"*Sigh no more, ladies, sigh no more,*
Men were deceivers ever,
One foot in sea, and one on shore,
To one thing constant never.
Then sigh not so, but let them go,

And be you blithe and bonny,
Converting all your sounds of woe
Into hey nonny nonny."

At other times, Sheila, Sally and Veronica would have laughed and applauded enthusiastically. Tonight, they kept silent.

"What, you don't like Balthasar's little ditty?" protested Janet. "You think that it is perhaps Much Ado About Nothing? I don't reckon so. Methinks, in fact, that a moral lies within which touches on you all. The men too," she practically shouted, jolting the husbands out of their discussion and predictions for the end of the match they wished they had been watching.

"Fred, my dear Will, pray tell us: Did anything you read in Ronald's diaries have any bearing, perhaps, on the silence of the present company of ladies?"

"Peter, John, George," said Will turning to the men. "Did you know that your wives were all shagging Janet's husband?

"Please give me some more trifle, Veronica," he added casually. "It's very good."

Will never got his second round of dessert.

Janet stood up, pulled him out of his chair, wished everyone a "good nonny, nonny" and took him straight out of the house.

Happily, Charles was still there, though they had to bang on the car window to awaken him. Behind the couple, he heard shouts and screams and, suspected Janet and Will, bowls of trifle hitting walls.

"Sounds like quite a party you've been having," Charles chuckled as he drove off and Janet began to recite:

"Tis now the very witching time of night,
When churchyards yawn and hell itself breathes out
Contagion to this world. Now could I drink hot blood,
And do such bitter business as the bitter day
Would quake to look on."

"Sorry, Madam, I think you've drunk quite enough hot blood for one evening," Will said in his sternest barman's voice. "Off to bed with you now."

CHAPTER TWENTY-ONE

"We killed Ronald," said Veronica.

"We think so, at least," said Sally.

"It wasn't the sleeping pills, in any case," said Sheila.

"I know," said Janet.

"You *do*?" asked Veronica.

"What about the box left by the body?" asked Sheila.

"Pathologists and coroners aren't *complete* idiots," said Janet. "Did you ever hear of autopsies, by any chance? When a man dies at that age there's an investigation of course. Blood analysis and so forth."

But wait a minute, thought Janet. Are they saying that they were in this together? That they were even there at his death? In *her* house?

The women had surrendered without discussion to her order that they should come and explain themselves and beg for the absolution that she had no intention at all of giving them. She had imagined that each had discovered her sisters in infidelity when Will had revealed the story at the party.

"Let's slow down the film a little," said Janet. "I haven't quite grasped the plot.

"Are you actually telling me that each of you knew that the other two were screwing Ronald?"

She looked at them one by one.

"Yes," said Veronica.

"Yes," said Sheila.

"Yes," said Sally.

"Ronald didn't know that we knew though," offered Veronica helpfully.

"Until the day of his death, that is," added Sally.

"You get more … more … more … *whorish* by the minute," said Janet with evident distaste, together with pleasure at finding the *mot juste* for these tarts.

"Look, Janet, we are all very sorry," said Sheila. "It's not a pretty story, we know."

Words temporarily failed Janet. She shook her head, snorted contemptuously, went to the kitchen, grabbed the gin and drank several huge gulps directly from the bottle. Feeling better and bolder, she quickly returned to the salon.

"Right. The story so far: The Gorgon sisters knew of each other's adulteries, but their victim did not know that they knew."

"I hardly think we can call Ronald a 'victim', Janet," Sally objected meekly.

"No, you're right. Bad choice of word. But anyhow, to continue: How long had these affairs been going on? How on earth did Ronald — and you, come to that — organize matters?"

"Do you really want to know all these things, Janet?" asked Sheila.

"Damn right I do. I shall drink your venom to the last drop."

The women did their best to explain. The affairs had begun within a few weeks of each other four or five months ago. It was in each case Ronald who had taken the initiative, had called them, had arranged meetings under the guise of talking to them privately about his marriage, had seduced them …

"'Seduced'?! Huh!" interrupted Janet. "I bet that was difficult! You trollops!"

"We didn't come here to be insulted, Janet," Veronica said mildly.

"Let her get it out of her system," said Sheila.

Janet ignored them both.

"So, when and where did these trysts take place?"

"I was Mondays," said Sally.

"Me, Wednesdays," said Sheila.

"Fridays," said Veronica.

"And where?"

"Here," said Sally.

"In this house? Under my roof? In the home of your closest friend? In my bed?"

"On the sofa in Ronald's study, actually," said Sally. "It converts."

"I bet it does, you harlots! And all that time I was at the publishers, reading manuscripts and making tea for authors … So, which of you is going to tell me how this sordid, odious, despicable tale ends?"

The three women looked at each other. Veronica volunteered.

"It was Friday, as you know. 'My' day, of course. I thought we might play a joke on Ronald and all show up together."

"How very droll," said Janet with evident revulsion.

"I have to say here, Janet, since you insist on knowing everything, that Ronald had been failing a little in his duties to his mistresses. Perhaps our charm was wearing off, we don't know.

"Anyhow, on our way here we dropped into a chemists and persuaded this nice young man to sell us a box of Viagra under the counter."

"We only wanted to tease Ronald a little," said Sally. "To tell him that if he couldn't handle three women, perhaps he should choose just one of us — or begin to take the pills."

"He was astonished to see all of us turn up together," Veronica resumed. "He really didn't know what to say. In any case, he brought out a lot of bottles and we began drinking. Rather too much, actually. We were quickly tipsy, to put it mildly, and brought out the Viagra. Ronald grabbed the box, took out three or four pills, and dropped them into his whisky."

"We all began undressing," ventured Sheila.

"Please spare me that," protested Janet.

"But then it was all over," said Veronica. "He threw down his drink in one gulp …"

"Began breathing with difficulty," added Sally.

"Clutched his chest," added Sheila.

"Tried to get up and collapsed on the floor," Veronica completed.

"He was gone," said Sheila.

"We tried his pulse, tried pumping on his chest, even mouth-to-mouth, but it was clearly all over, nothing to do. We understood straight away he'd had heart failure."

"You called an ambulance, of course?" asked Janet sardonically.

"We should have. Yes, we should have", said Veronica. "But he looked so very dead."

"You're experts, of course," said Janet.

There was silence. Each of the women looked at her shoes and ardently wished she were elsewhere.

Janet stared in front of her and thought nothing at all.

After three or four long minutes, she addressed them all:

"I should call the police, you know. I could have you all jailed for manslaughter at the very least. But tell me, what did you do then?"

"We panicked, basically," said Veronica. "We saw a box of sleeping pills by Ronald's couch; we emptied it and stuffed the pills into our pockets, then placed it by the body; we cleaned the glasses and put them away, together with the bottles."

"Then we ran for it," said Sheila. "You called us that evening to tell us that you had found Ronald dead when you came home from the office. And that was that."

"Until your friend read Ronald's diaries," said Sally. "What's his name, by the way? 'Colonel Frederick Acton' …"

"Will."

Janet wondered if she should indeed call the police. She had to think quickly. What would I gain from it? Nothing, except humiliation. Her story would end up in the *Daily Mail*, for sure, and that was the absolutely worst fate that could ever befall any cheated woman. They would be laughing at her in every hypocritical, bigoted, frustrated home in the country. Only the no-less-wretched *Sun* would be honest, she thought. She saw the headline already: "Bonking Banker Banged Bitches, Claims Widow."

No, she would not take the matter further. All she wanted was to see the back of these traitorous women forever and to go away with Will.

She had one last thought.

"How did your dear husbands take the news?"

"They've left us for a week or two," said Sheila.

"They had 'to get away'," said Sally.

"To 'think it over'," said Veronica.

"To 'put their lives back together'," added Sheila.

"To 'find forgiveness in their hearts', or so they said," added Sally.

"So they've all gone off to Wales," Veronica informed her.

"They took their fishing rods," Sheila said.

What none of the women knew at that moment was that in midweek Arsenal had an away game against Swansea …

Throwing her ex-friends out of the house, Janet called after them: "*Though those that are betray'd do feel the treason sharply, yet the traitor stands in worse case of woe.*"

She hoped Imogen was right.

CHAPTER TWENTY-TWO

"Strumpf was crying in Will's arms.

"Mein Gott, I shall miss you," wept the old man. "My only freund in zis hostile nation."

"Come on, Sigmund, don't be unfair, England has been very good to you."

Strumpf wiped his tears on Will's shirt collars and began to expatiate on his cruel fate at the hands of the belligerent natives. His friend quickly interrupted him.

"Sigmund, sit down, won't you? I have things to fix and guests to attend to. We'll speak later."

Strumpf did as he was told and retired to the bar couch with a mug of slivovitz. Mike sat down next to him.

"Hello Svengali."

"Hello Marlowe."

They both laughed and clinked their glass and mug together.

"Vy you call me 'Svengali', zough?"

"You told me to—at the funeral party."

"Ah yes, I vas a leetle, vot you say, sozzled?"

"Yes, that you were certainly," confirmed Mike. "But tell me, how do you do it?"

"Zat's easy, just vatch," said Strumpf, downing a great slug of brandy.

"No, not get drunk—hypnotize people."

"Vot?"

"Tell me, Sigmund, it's all a sham, trickery, isn't it?"

Strumpf looked suddenly defeated, emptied, spent. Unmasked. He sighed deeply.

"So, you know about zat, about ze show. How you find out?"

"We have our ways, Sigmund. But don't worry about that. I'd just like to learn a little more. Professional curiosity, you could call it."

"Mike, I vill tell you. But von condition, plees. You never tell Vill about zis. Promise me."

"Of course, of course," Mike lied. He had already told Will, of course. "Mum's the word."

"Mum is vot?" said a puzzled Strumpf.

"The cat will remain in the bag," said Mike helpfully.

"I understand nozing. Mums and cats, can't you speak ozer than in riddles?"

"It means that I shall keep quiet about your secret life. I shan't breathe a word to Will or anybody else."

"Vielen Dank, my friend, vielen Dank ... Vell, yes, I am a fake in my real life also, it's true. Zere is nozing real about vot I do; ze hypnotic trance is a delusion, I vill not say ze contrary."

"So how do you pull it off, Sigmund? There are laws about these things. Why haven't you been arrested as an impostor?"

"I am a showman, Mike, first of all. Everysing depends on zat. Lots of yokes, of course. And trust. You cannot believe how veak people are in ze mind department and vant to trust me. It is beyond imagination!"

"Well, I have a few ideas about psychology too, Sigmund, you know. But go on."

"Vell, people vill believe anyzing, absolutely anyzing, even about zemselves. You can suggest vot you like and zey vill svallow it. It all depends zat I pick ze right people from ze audience. I can see zem a mile off, as you say. Zey are eager; zey *vant* to join ze show; zey *vant* to do what I ask; zey *vant* me to take over zere minds; zey vant to be fooled!—Don't you sink ve are doomed, Mike?" Strumpf interrupted himself gravely.

"You and me?"

"Nein, nein. Ze human race. Ve simply cannot get people to sink for zemselves. I haf a compatriot, you know, who vonce hypnotized millions, tens of millions! Zings haf not got any better since zen!"

Will had put on some jazzy music and was dancing with Fat Mary, the affectionate nickname he used, with her consent, for his former client, who had become reconciled with her sister and sworn an undying bond of gratitude to him.

"She vone beeg handful, nein?" Strumpf remarked to Mike, nodding towards the smooching couple.

"She gets more attractive by the minute," said Mike, raising his glass and banging it against Strumpf's mug once more.

"From zis moment, everysing I say to you, every single vord I say to you , however stupid, vill instantly become your reality. You vill do vot I ask," said Strumpf staring into Mike's eyes.

"Knock it off, Sigmund, you're making me feel

dizzy. But tell me, why do you go around claiming that you're a psychoanalyst? That's even more disreputable than being a hypnotist, isn't it?"

"I vonce vas such a man, a very long time ago. In ze gut old days, ven zere vas much respect for us. You can imagine vot a success I vas, a disciple of ze great Freud, straight off ze train from Vienna … Ze ladies vere crazy to come tell me zere wildest fantasies. I cannot even repeat vot I hear. You vould not believe it!"

"Having a good time?" asked Will, planting Mary at the bar again and sitting down with them on the couch.

"Yes, great thanks," said Mike. "Very good idea to organize this parting shindig for us. Who are all these people?"

"A few Extra! clients like Mary over there with whom I had a good time on assignment. I kept in touch, despite the rules."

Mike smiled and wagged his finger in reprimand.

"And some of the customers here I have liked the most over the last couple of years. People I shall miss, like you two. Most of them are lonely souls, otherwise they wouldn't be here, I guess," Will reflected. "Potential Extra! clients all of them. Look at Dan, for instance."

He pointed to the New Zealander, who was demonstrating an All Blacks attacking move to a yawning Mary with his empty beer glasses lined up on the bar.

"And Alwyn over there, sitting as usual in deadly silence. He takes time to warm up, but he'll be singing 'Land of My Fathers' before the night's over, I'm sure, while he dreams of the valleys. And a lovely voice he has too, like most of the Welsh."

As Will cast around for another customer to identify, Strumpf broke into an ecstatic smile and clapped his hands in joy. He had spied four ladies of his acquaintance, members of a certain Nigerian dance company, saunter into the bar laughing and joking.

"Will, vot a good idea to invite ze beauties! I sink you sink of me, ja?"

"Ja, ja, ja," laughed Will. "I told them that you would be here, Sigmund, and they promised to drop by on the way home. I'm glad you're pleased.

"You don't look exactly distressed either, Mike. But please behave yourself."

At that, Will got up to greet the ladies and to prepare drinks for them.

With the help of champagne and Strumpf's pleas, they were soon coerced into dancing, despite their protests of fatigue after the evening's ballet performance.

As the party raged on, Will thought of Janet and his love for her. He was glad she had declined to come that evening, too busy preparing for their voyage. Things might change in time—who knew?—but for the moment he was greedy to have her only for himself, to be alone as much as possible. He knew she would have other ideas, but he could live with that. Her happiness was now his goal, infinitely superior to his own ambitions, of that he had not the slightest doubt. *Il n'y a pas d'amour, il n'y a que des preuves d'amour*, the French poets had said. Well, perhaps his desperate need to make *her* happy rather than himself was the greatest proof of all of his love, he thought.

"So, you got the dame," said Mike, coming up later to the bar where Will was beginning to clear up as the first guests began to drift away. "I could have you fired, you know."

Will laughed happily. "I was just thinking of her, actually."

"Quite a dame, quite a dame," repeated Mike. There was simply nothing else to say about the sensational Mrs Chapman.

"One for the road, boss?" asked Will.

"I think not, thanks. I think I should get Houdini home," he said, pointing at a slouched Strumpf on the couch. "And then myself. I have a new candidate coming in at nine. You're leaving quite a big hole, my boy. I need another star act."

"How about last confessions?" suggested Mike, now standing in the doorway holding Strumpf more or less erect in his arms.

"OK, Father Fielding."

"I was never a detective. It was just a dream. I made it up."

"Who followed Sigmund?"

"One of the Extra! operatives. One of your colleagues."

"Well, I never …"

"And you, Will? What do you have to confess as you

stand on the threshold of your new life? Come out with it!"

"Nothing, Mike. Nothing at all, I'm afraid. I'm the straight guy, remember? The last honest man left standing."

As Mike lurched into the night, arm in arm with a barely conscious Strumpf, he was heard to yell, for the information of the residents of Islington and perhaps beyond: "*To be honest, as this world goes, is to be one man picked out of ten thousand!*"

"And I, Marlowe, picked him!" he bellowed. "My boy Will. There will never be another like him."

It was so late, the neighborhood didn't even protest. If there were other honest folk around, they were sound asleep.

CHAPTER TWENTY-THREE

Two days later, Will and Janet smiled lovingly and wordlessly at each other while the Eurostar pulled out of St Pancras station in rain and light mist, bound for their new life in France.

Journeys should always begin in silence, thought Janet. She was so happy that Will too found it unnecessary to speak. These little concords are the stuff of which lasting love is made, she reflected confidently.

Silence is the perfectest herald of joy, she whispered to him in her heart, *as you are mine, I am yours, I give away myself for you and dote upon the exchange.*

"I heard again from Mike last night," said Will after a long moment. "This will make you laugh—he's put Strumpf 'on the payroll', as they say in the movies."

"What an earth for?"

"He hasn't figured it out yet. But he's convinced there must be a use for a hypnotist, even a fake, at Extra! He just has to find the right 'product'. I'm sure that his imagination is already working overtime, sifting through the options of what's feasible, what's needed 'in the market', and what's more or less legal."

Janet threw back her red head gaily and laughed with abandon.

As they left London's endless suburbs behind them and glimpsed the first fields of Kent, Janet put her hand upon his and squeezed it.

"Will darling, just make me one promise."

"Of course, sweetheart."

"Let's never stop lying to each other."

"Never, my love."

"But please, only lie to me about the *important* things. About how beautiful I look in the morning as I awake; about how you always *adore* what I wear; about how no one has ever had such good taste when choosing your shirts; about how I never age. Lie that you want to go dancing with me every night of our lives; lie that my wit is simply the sharpest you ever heard; lie that I really do not drink too much.

"There will be no need to lie about our pasts, of course, because we shall never talk about them, shall we?" she added.

"No, my love. *What's past is prologue; what to come, in yours and my discharge.*"

"Wonderful, Will, simply wonderful!" said Janet ecstatically. "It cannot ever have been better said, ever. Blessèd Shakespeare! The script is indeed only ours now to write.

"But what lies would you like me to tell to *you*, dear, dear Will?"

"Just call me 'colonel' from time to time, especially in public, would you? My military career was far too brief—one lunch and a couple of dinners, as you know—and I enjoyed it more than you can possibly imagine. It gave me a sense of self-importance that I've never otherwise experienced in my whole life."

He raised his chin and gave a smart, sharp salute; Janet flicked her temple with one finger in reply.

In time, the train emerged from the underwater tunnel into blinding French sunshine and blue skies full of seagulls.

"*Sweet bodements!*" cheered Janet.

And after a while:

"Will, may I show my tits on the beach? Just once?"

"Janet, darling, you can show your arse, if it pleases you. I don't mind," he lied.

This is my man, she thought to herself.

"Will, when we've danced ourselves to exhaustion at the guinguettes on the Marne and in the cellars of the Latin Quarter; when we've drunk and feasted ourselves to satiety at Pierre Gagnaire, Taillevent, Le Grand Vefour and other, new places we haven't even heard of; when we've scaled the Eiffel Tower on foot just for the view; when we've emptied the bookshops of Saint-Germain-des-Prés; had a glass or two with Hemingway's ghost at the Closerie des Lilas; when we've done the Riviera from end to end and beyond; when we've run with the bulls in Pamplona—don't frown, Will, few men are actually killed; taken martinis at the Maria Christina in San Sebastián; sung with Basque choirs in the squares of Saint Jean de Luz; when we've done all that and much, much, more, I think I'd actually like to try a slow, calm, peaceful life together. I could never imagine that I would say this, but it seems to me right now that this is what I shall want. When we gain a freedom so long desired, I can imagine well that in time

our yearnings change again. That was very philosophical, wasn't it Will?

"And by the way, we've never talked about it, thank
God, but I have stacks and stacks and stacks of money,
the ill-gotten gains of ten years of banking, and, if you
really love me, Will, you will never, ever mention the
subject. Just be happy, that's all I want.

"So, do you have ideas, darling, even now, about this
slow life to which we might like to retreat, even temporarily, when we are breathless from fun and play?"

Will smiled, overwhelmed with love for this truly
remarkable, beautiful woman and astonished anew that
she should have sealed her future and fate with *him*, of
all people, and proposed timidly:

"We might set up a snail farm in Burgundy. You
can't get a slower life than that, I think."

Janet pulled him across the narrow table and hugged
him in joy. "Snails! Of course, we shall become snails!"

But as their train slipped silently into the Gare du
Nord, the sun cascading down upon them through its
glass and iron roof, she had one immediate desire only.

"Will, before we do anything else at all, can we go
and see Sartre's waiter?"

"Of course, my love, I'm quite sure that he's expecting us."

ABOUT THE AUTHOR

Born in 1954 in London of mixed Scottish and English parentage, Timothy Balding grew up and was educated on a British military base in Germany. He left school and his family at the age of sixteen to return alone to the United Kingdom, where he was hired as a reporter on local newspapers in Reading in the county of Berkshire. For the ensuing decade, he worked on local and regional titles and then at Press Association, the national news agency, covering politics in Westminster, the British Parliament. He exiled himself to Paris, France, in 1980, and spent the next thirty years working for international, non-governmental organizations. For twenty-five of these, he was Chief Executive Officer of the World Association of Newspapers, the representative global group of media publishers and editors, established after World War II to defend the freedom and independence of the press worldwide. A Knight (First Class) in the Order of the White Rose of Finland—an honor accorded him by Nobel Peace laureate Martti Ahtisaari, former Finnish President—Timothy Balding currently lives in the Basque region of France and devotes himself to writing. *The Impostors* is his second novel.

ALSO AVAILABLE FROM UWSP

- *On Dialogic Speech* by L. P. Yakubinsky
- *Passing Time: An Essay on Waiting* by Andrea Köhler
- *In Praise of Weakness* by Alexandre Jollien
- *Vase of Pompeii: A Play* by Lajos Walder
- *Below Zero: A Play* by Lajos Walder
- *Tyrtaeus: A Tragedy* by Lajos Walder
- *The Complete Plays* by Lajos Walder
- *Homo Conscius: A Novel* by Timothy Balding
- *Spanish Light: A Novel* by Stephen Grant
- *On Language & Poetry* by L. P. Yakubinsky
- *Philosophical Truffles* by Michael Eskin
- *The Complete Poems* by Lajos Walder (Bilingual Edition)
- *Összes Versei* by Vándor Lajos
- *Of Parents and Children: Tools for Nurturing a Lifelong Relationship* by Jorge & Demián Bucay
- *The Man Who Couldn't Stop Thinking: A Novel* by Timothy Balding